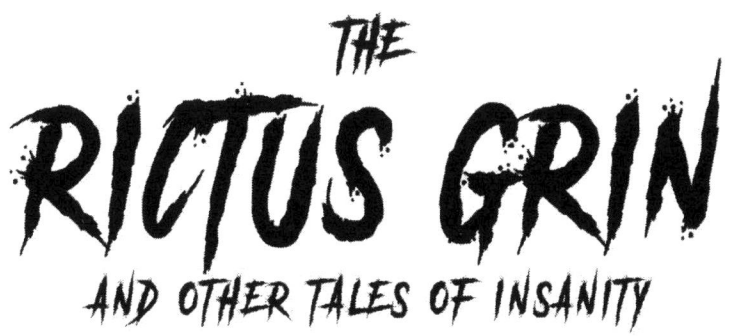

THE RICTUS GRIN

AND OTHER TALES OF INSANITY

ERICA SUMMERS

THE
RICTUS GRIN
AND OTHER TALES OF INSANITY

More by Erica Summers

Books:
Writhe

Vanity Kills

Mantis

Bad God's Tower

Anthologies:
Price Slashers *(Slashic Horror Press)*

Ensuring Your Place in Hell II *(Splatploitation)*

Anthology of Splatterpunk *(Hellbound Books)*

AIR *(Eerie River Publishing)*

It Calls From Below *(Eerie River Publishing)*

TABLE OF CONTENTS

For Dave and Heather…
My muses. My best friends.
The two loves of my life.

AN INTRODUCTION BY

CHISTO HEALY

Like many of you, probably, I stumbled upon Erica Summers. It was every bit happenstance and a moment I'll be forever grateful for.

I am someone who believes strongly in community. I believe even if you write the most depraved horror in the world, you should spread positivity and uplift people off of the page. The universe exists through balance. If I were a cartoon, my catchphrase would be, "We're all in this together."

With this in mind, when someone is looking for a beta reader, an ARC reader, someone to blurb their cover, etc., I always volunteer unless I'm completely swamped with deadlines, but sometimes, even then, because I'm a professional at spreading myself thin. I'm also a professional at spreading cold, unmelted butter. It's a skill.

Anyway, one day, an author I had never read was looking for other authors to read and blurb her book, *Bad God's Tower*. To be truthful, I wasn't expecting much. I don't set the bar too high because I like happy surprises more than disappointment. *Bad God's Tower* was every bit the happy surprise. I was giddy enough to break out the pompoms, which doesn't happen often, even if I look good in a skirt.

I've always enjoyed pulp and often write it myself, but I am eternally in love with beautiful prose. When someone like Simon Clark can write horror with the poetic beauty of literature, it has always stood above the rest for me. That was the first thing I noticed about Erica's writing. The phrasing was delicate, purposeful, poignant, and concise. I found myself re-reading sentences just to appreciate the elegance. I was floored and immediately jealous. Imagine the cartoon version of me again, shaking my pencil and shouting, "How does she do it?!"

As I read on, I discovered the characters were full of life and vibrancy. The story was compelling. The horror was visceral, frightening, and intense. Nothing was sacrificed for the creation of that gorgeous prose.

It was all there, complete.

I delivered my blurb and found that Ms. Summers was as humble and easy to talk to as she was talented. The more we talked, the more I realized just how similar we were as people. We have a lot of shared life experiences, even if some were the type to inspire a horror novel.

So, not only did I find my favorite horror author of the last decade, but I also found a friend. A real one to boot, not just another candy-coated participation trophy friend.

That said, I enjoy both candy and trophies.

Still, Erica and I have helped each other by being the type of friend who is honest rather than doused in sugar.

I'll pause here for a moment while you sing Def Leppard to yourself.

We have dared say, "Yeah, bud… this part of your story doesn't work," and it's made us better. We have vented frustrations and shared goals, pushed each other to achieve, and continue to support each other to this day. We have a book together now through Slashic Horror Press with Mick Collins called *Price Slashers* that hit number one in three different categories.

Erica is someone I respect as a colleague and as a human. That's why I was honored when she came to me and asked me to write an introduction to her collection.

It also made perfect sense.

I've read everything Erica has written and plan to read everything she writes as long as I'm on this earth. When you turn the page and dig into this collection, you will understand why. You will see the wordsmith in action. You will see her range, the variety of sub-genres she can fearlessly tackle, and how personal and real her horror can be. From crazy mothers to dangerous machines, frightening churches to monsters, and everything in between, you're in for one hell of a ride.

Thank you for accompanying me on this exciting and horrific journey of exploration into the warped mind of my close friend, the masterful Erica Summers.

See you on the other side,

Chisto Healy,
Author of *Two of a Kind* & *The Gateway in Apartment 8*

It was just a hole. Just a small, never-ending cavity snaking down like a drainpipe in the center of a massive, arid Wyoming plot of farmland. Just a hole sucking all the life and joy from John Mitchell, along with the occasional piss of rainwater, down into the earth's crust.

The field was rotten. That's what they'd said. But John hadn't been inclined to believe the verbal diarrhea from chattering small-town idiots. Not until he'd witnessed it with his own bloodshot eyes. It wasn't until he himself, smelled the overwhelming metallic twinge of copper wafting up from the wretched soil as if trucks of dirt had been dumped atop a plane of filthy pennies.

The ground was sour. They'd said that, too. That concept never really sunk in until John and the kids settled in that first summer and watched their crops – their livelihood – wither, shrivel, and rot in a pestilent slow-motion nightmare.

Things had changed, though. Tall corn stalks, like green worshippers with outstretched hands, celebrated the overhead sun. A mob of plentiful sugar beets flourished, springing forth lush, healthy foliage in perfect rows above each root crop. The loud gasps of abundant, swishing wheat around him meant things had turned around.

But at what cost?

John shuddered at the price he'd paid for the abundant accumulation of lumbering plants encircling him now, towering overhead like bloodthirsty bullies with mayhem and chaos coursing through thick stalks. He felt like an outnumbered soldier losing ground to an enemy aching to fully overtake. His soul was strangled by their wicked little roots. Their infinite tangle of tendrils squeezed his chest with crushing guilt that grew as exponentially as they did every woeful day.

And yet...

There he was again. *Bleeding.*

Listlessly standing above the hole. *That ungodly hole.*

He wavered in the dusky country sky above a hole he wished he'd never uncovered. John would give any earthly possession to go backward, knowing all he'd sacrifice for this corrupted patch of the earth.

He never would've lifted that stack of hay, no doubt placed purposefully to muffle the feverish whispering seeping from the ground.

No matter how much straw John had ever tried to mound back on it, it was never enough to suffocate the voice.

John had been relieved. He hadn't heard the whispering for days. It was as if the thing at the other end was, for once, content with the offerings bestowed upon it.

But John could make out His faint whispers now…

Asking John for the world again in His horribly indescribable tone, a voice that rattled around in John's thick, tired skull, ordering him to obey once again.

Like he had a choice.

***

A bad seed. That's what Janice's mother had called her — or rather, screamed at her — as she barreled down a long stretch of back roads in the

9

ratty teal sedan. It was time for Mom to pawn her off on her relatives. It only seemed fair. After all, Janice had been "dumped on her" when Andrew took off for the older, homelier secretary. She felt it was within her right to hot-potato the difficult teen elsewhere so Lynn could "have her life back." She figured a laborious summer on the farm would do Janice's attitude wonders.

"Get your goddamn feet off the dash," Lynn growled through gritted teeth.

Janice glared and slunk into the passenger seat, following orders reluctantly. She slid her bare feet back into flip-flops and tugged out her phone.

"No bars. How am I supposed to call if I need anything?" Her voice was low and sullen. With a middle finger, she flicked away from her face a chin-length tendril of amateur-dyed lavender hair.

"Your uncle's got a landline."

"Ugh. How'll I text my friends?"

"Sounds like your problem, not mine."

"Nothing ever is," Janice smarted off.

"Oh yeah, I'm living the high life now." Lynn's voice seethed angry sarcasm. After a moment of silence, she flipped her mood, suddenly trying to seem as if she gave a fraction of a damn. "Maybe Ellis and Andrea can introduce you to some of their friends."

"Ellis is a frickin' nerd. That kid's got no friends," Janice protested.

"Never know, you haven't seen him or Andrea in five years." Lynn stared at the road. She pursed two hot pink chapped lips together and tousled her bleach-fried blond mane.

"Not since the funeral." The words brought back memories of how Janice had morbidly double-dog-dared her little sister to glimpse the allegedly gory remains inside the miniature closed casket. "Who knows? They're probably all meth heads or something by now, for all we know."

"You'll probably fit in just fine then, little miss spliff."

"Are you kidding? It was a joint! One. That's nowhere close to the same as meth." Janice picked at her thumbnail, flaking the metallic chrome polish.

Lynn glared at Janice, catching a glimpse of the scars on the young girl's inner thigh. Perfectly parallel self-inflicted razor lines. They reminded her of tidy rows of crops they were passing now.

"Maybe with all the work they'll have you doing, you'll be so busy you won't have the time for cutting. You know, idle hands and all that bullshit."

"What do you even care? If I sliced my fucking throat and it'd take you three days to realize it."

"Jesus Christ, watch your fucking language! You know, I'm working damn hard on this Bachelor's, Janice. You think it's easy? Think it's easy being a single mom saddled with three kids I didn't even want?"

"Real nice." Janice rolled her eyes. "And Mother of the Year award goes to..."

"It's true! Your dad wanted you! I didn't get a choice in the matter. I was just his goddamned incubator." Lynn's martyrdom abruptly halted as she slowed to a crawl at a dusty wooden sign jostling in a gust of whipping wind:

Mitchell Farms Welcomes You.

Lynn turned in, exhilarated by the notion that, within the hour, she'd be a hundred and twenty pounds lighter.

***

As Lynn neared the house at the end of the lingering dirt driveway, Marsha trickled into view. She was kneeling on a foam pad in the in-ground flower bed butted against a rickety porch. Marsha caressed a patch of superb Siberian irises. In an otherwise terracotta-colored landscape, the fully-bloomed flowers were intense blasts of blue and yellow vivaciousness.

Lynn observed the woman mouthing words silently, assuming she was singing along to something in headphones obscured by wisps of brittle brunette hair.

Otherwise, why else wouldn't Marsha be aware of the racket behind her?

Audible a half-mile away, Lynn's car was slowly rattling to its looming permanent death, one violent engine knock and whirl at a time.

Lynn killed the engine and anxiously thrust herself from the driver's seat, craving blood flow. Once out, she primped the overgrown black roots in her bleach-blonde hair with her fingertips and swung her hands theatrically in an attempt to catch Marsha's eye.

Finally, it worked. Marsha peered up languidly.

Lynn was caught off-guard. From Marsha's once-youthful, always-smiling face, it seemed now all effervescence had been drained. She was pale and sheathed in a thin layer of sweat, which made her once-supple skin look anemic and sick. She seemed more like a decrepit, sunken shell of Marsha's former self.

Inside, Lynn wanted to laugh. In just five years, her sister-in-law had aged terribly. She closed her gaping mouth as a nicety.

The haggard woman rose to her feet, unsteady, offering a look of confusion.

"Heyyyyyy, Marsha!" Suddenly, Lynn was animated and silly. It was the most playful Janice had seen her in so long, and the source of the sudden joy was obvious.

Janice couldn't wait to be rid of her, either.

Marsha stared at Lynn, pensive and befuddled. "Do I...?" Her voice was as weak as her color. The savage contrast in their levels of energy was unnerving.

"It's Lynn." She was insulted and alarmed. "You know... John's sister?"

Nothing. No spark of recognition.

"Marsha, I was in your wedding, for God's sake."

Marsha feigned a look of understanding. "Of course. Lynn."

As Janice lugged a green suitcase from the trunk, Marsha's joyless, hazy eyes drifted to the girl.

"Do you remember Janice?" Lynn's voice forced an uncomfortable laugh.

The cognition failed again.

There was something not quite right about Marsha's eyes.

They were lifeless.

Like they'd been replaced with scuffed, acrylic versions by a skilled taxidermist. With both hands clasped around the top strap, Janice hopped the overstuffed suitcase to the patio and planted it in the dirt like a signpost.

"Where are the kids, Marsha?" Lynn craned her neck in an attempt to make some headway with the woman, clearly experiencing a bout of bewildering senility. She wasn't sure how early something like dementia could present. Marsha was just fifty-one, only a decade older than Lynn.

Marsha cocked her pallid face sideways in a jarring motion and studied Lynn, baffled by every word.

"Marsha, where's John?" Lynn spoke slowly as if the unhinged woman was deaf.

She couldn't help but notice that her sister-in-law wasn't wearing any earbuds.

A hint of a smile crept across Marsha's face. "Oh. John."

"Yes, John. Where's John, Marsha?"

"He's probably by the hole again." She grinned, wider now. Through the years, her teeth had become as translucent and unnatural-looking as her deficient flesh.

Lynn's face soured. "What hole, Marsha?"

Marsha snapped her head around as if she'd been caught doing something inappropriate. She scuttled around the yard in abrupt, hesitant movements, much like a frightened chicken. Lynn's eyes traced down Marsha's disgustingly thin arms and settled on something she'd failed to observe earlier:

Marsha's left hand was bloody.

Small, red streams spread out from a gash below the crook of her arm like a crusted fisherman's map of some tangled southern bayou.

As John emerged from behind a filthy once-crimson tractor across the front yard, Marsha drifted back down to her knees in a trance.

John's dress habits were exactly how Lynn remembered. He wore the same old shabby bib overalls and a Swiss-cheesed navy-blue tank beneath. His ripped boots were encrusted with mud and fertilizer.

"John, there you are! Marsha cut herself," Lynn blurted, hating herself for the instant reversion to her tattle-tale little sister role.

John half-glanced over and then calmly returned his gaze to Lynn. "She's fine. Cuts herself in the garden all the time. We all do. This land doesn't give back 'less you give it some blood, sweat, and tears first." His big brother nonchalance was typical.

John always offered solutions to injuries like rub a little dirt on it and quit cryin'.

"Losing some weight, I see." Lynn's tone was a complimentary way to mask the truth, which was that John had lost a nauseating amount of weight. He looked like he'd been caged and starved. "Marsha's cookin' gone downhill?"

John laughed. "Nah. It's this place. Takes it outta you. 'Specially when you're short-handed."

"Well, have I got the solution for you!" Lynn's voice was loud, like a carnival barker. She motioned to her daughter.

"'At's right! Come up from Denver to live with us for a stretch?" John wrapped a dirty, emaciated arm around her.

"I guess." Janice shrugged.

Like she had a choice.

"It ain't gonna be easy. There's lots to do. We're gonna keep you busy. Idle hands..." John smiled.

Janice smirked at the sibling's almost-rehearsed phrasing of that old saying.

"Everything copacetic with Marsha?" Lynn got close, quiet. "Is she...?"

John's face contorted into a remorseful expression. "She has her good days and her bad.

It's tough sometimes." John suddenly scooped Lynn up and hugged his sister. "It's good to see you, Ducky."

Lynn smacked him harder than she intended. "Don't friggin' call me that!" She giggled and added, "Jerk."

Janice prodded for more intel. "Why doesn't she like being called Ducky?"

Lynn pointed a finger at John and threatened jokingly. "Don't you goddamned tell her a thing!" She laughed, checked her watch, and then headed back toward the car. "Thanks for taking Jan for a bit. I just… can't…with her."

"Aw, she's just young and feisty, just like you when you were that age." He turned his pale, sunken eyes to Janice and smiled. "Don't worry. You ain't gonna wanna leave this place when Ducky comes to get you in the fall."

John's humor was as dry as the dirt beneath them. Janice frowned and stared down at the suitcase.

Lynn giggled and slid a foot on the floorboard. "Hell, John, if she wants to stay, you can keep her."

***

Janice had unpacked before the powdery dirt from Lynn's Colorado-bound tires even settled. She hadn't brought much: all the summer-appropriate clothes she owned, a borrowed hardback of angsty poetry, a zippered sack of toiletries, hair dye, and her phone, a useless electronic link to the outside world. Two percent battery remained.

Junior's room had an ominous feel. It was still decorated with sun-faded wallpaper sporting artsy examples of various dinosaurs in a tight, dizzying pattern. A plastic pterodactyl hung from a J-hook by fishing string, soaring above the bed like the winged protector to the being slumbering beneath. A row of brontosauruses craned their rubbery necks in various angles atop a shelf, book-ended by a poorly sculpted clay velociraptor and an ornate T-Rex piggy bank, their colorful paint jobs muted with a tragic layer of thick dust.

Janice plopped down on the comforter displaying a faded cross-sectioned volcano spewing lava, its inner layers all labeled. On the bedside table, she spied a lamp with a real fossil base composed of a cracked-in-half rock. She traced its cord down to the packed outlet, yanked the plug for the light, and replaced it with her phone charger. A wash of relief swept over her as the lightning bolt indicator flashed brightly across the scuffed screen. Despite the lack of service, her brightly colored game apps would provide her with a little taste of home out in Bum-fuck Egypt.

A wooden floorboard creaked in the hallway outside of the open door. Janice's heart leaped, and sudden panic slapped her.

Andrea stood in the doorway. Janice hadn't seen her cousin in half a decade, but she recognized her instantly despite her bizarre appearance.

"Jesus! You scared the hell out of me!" Janice laughed, clutching her pounding chest.

Andrea didn't say anything.

She lingered there, feeble arms stiff by her sides. Her shoulder-width feet sat at the base of two scarred legs rife with wide, galactic bruises.

She was malnourished. Filthy. Her jean shorts were grungy, and her mud-smudged t-shirt was tea-colored despite being once white. She looked like she'd waded through a swamp and then had been forced to dry that way.

And the look on her face...

Her dispirited expression was chilling. The girl's brown eyes were insipid.

"You're in Junior's room." Her eerie voice was as cold as her dead expression.

"I know. John told me this is where I should sleep while I'm here," Janice said, her smile fading subconsciously with Andrea's stoicism. "I'm your cousin. Don't you... remember me?"

"You never should have come here." Andrea's voice was a flat whisper.

No shit, Sherlock.

Janice wanted to laugh at the comment but instead was as still and silent as the teen in the hallway. As she stared, she realized Andrea hadn't blinked those blank eyes in a while...

Possibly their whole interaction.

First Aunt Marsha, now her?

"You shouldn't stay in his room," Andrea warned, her head cocked sideways. The movement was jerky, almost mechanical.

"Well, where should I sleep then?" Janice threw her hands up defensively.

"You can't stay in this room," she repeated with a stiff shrug.

Janice scoffed, preparing for a potential altercation. Despite Andrea being two years older and at least a foot taller, Janice knew with the rail-thin state of her scrawny body that she would be the victor if it came to blows.

"Tines... won't like it," Andrea muttered hypnotically.

Janice was genuinely confused. "Who's Tines?"

Did they have a pet that she hadn't met yet? Or a foreign exchange student, perhaps? To her knowledge, there was no one in the family by that name.

As placidly as she'd appeared, Andrea trod off down the hall. With every sluggish, precise step, her bare, soiled feet caressed the squalid floorboards.

***

Suppertime. This was something Janice didn't have much experience with at home. Lynn had buried herself in community college course material since the divorce, leaving Janice and her siblings to fend for themselves at mealtime. Lynn was typically so engulfed in test prep worksheets that she often forgot about cooking or the fact that she even had children. Despite claiming to be a "stay-at-home-mom" cruising off Andrew's hefty alimony checks, her spawn had essentially become unsupervised latchkey children, defaulting Janice to the lead position of power in their newfound Lord-of-the-Flies-type hierarchy. She found herself regularly inventing soups out of watered-down condiments, nuking bowls of Ramen, or splitting microwave TV dinners with her underlings as they crowded around the small flat-screen in the room she shared with her sister.

Not... this.

Janice sat, famished, at the oak dinner table in the drab little dining room on the first floor. Like everything else in the house, the room felt out of date and decrepit. Long, tacky tobacco-colored strips hung down like brown stalagmites from the ceiling, its real estate completely packed with dead or dying flies. The room had a distinct, low buzz to it, like paper shreds caught in an oscillating fan, from the tiny, terrified little wings vibrating out of sync.

The middle of the hefty table bore a bountiful spread of delectable-looking food, the scents of which made Janice's growling empty stomach flip. Around her, Marsha, John, and their children, Andrea and Ellis, sat quietly, slender hands clasped upon hers for prayer.

Nothing seemed right with any of them.

They were pitted and sallow. They seemed like some sort of half-broken, colorless carnival ride drained of all vitality. Frail arms adjoined by tangles of bony hands. The family felt like an out-of-order fleshy carousel composed of blanched, sickly extremities. Janice didn't want to touch any of them. Especially to say grace, something she had no use for at all as an atheist.

A renegade fly tore through the room, but they were unaffected by it — or maybe just wholly unaware or unresponsive. The buzzing pest landed like a microscopic plane using one of the steaming ears of corn tucked in an overflowing glass dish as a runway. John's voice was almost as quiet as the fly. As he spoke, his thin skin danced over the tendons and sinewy muscles of his throat.

"As promised, we have sacrificed our bounty to you, Tines. And you have sacrificed your bounty to us."

There was that name again.

Was he... praying to it?

"That is the way it always has been and the way it must always be." John clenched Janice's hand with force and then released it. Without so much as an "Amen," the bone-weary family jostled around the plates of steaming food like they only had mere seconds to eat. Dishes flew back and forth in front of Janice's ping-ponging eyes.

John snatched up a serving platter heaped high with steaming steaks and forked the largest, rarest slab of beef atop the mess of vegetables already slathered on the porcelain circle in front of him. He passed the platter, grabbed the steak with his bare hands, and shredded its sopping musculature like some ravenous animal, coating his teeth's shortbread shade a watery pink.

Marsha did the same with a buttered ear of corn, allowing the sloppy juices to run down her waxen face and the dried blood streams crusted to her forearms, gnawing at it recklessly with the right side of her molars like a raccoon. Ellis and Andrea both attacked freshly baked wheat rolls, cramming them into their apathetic faces as though they'd just heard the starting gun of an eating competition.

The family was so engaged in their dizzying primal feast that they hadn't seen Janice's judgemental green eyes gawking. She wanted to gag in disgust when she watched John wash his steak down with a quickly chugged glass of warm cow's milk. The glass contained a helpless fly swimming a panicked backstroke in it. John didn't seem to notice, sucking the fly right down.

"I guess… you guys really build up an appetite working out here." Her words were obvious and smug and still, somehow, laden with fear. She wondered how such feeble people could have appetites this voracious.

"Don't skimp on the steak. You need the iron." John edged the slabs of beef her way with his greasy, soot-smeared forearm. His kind, peaky face glistened with fats and juices as he smiled. "After dinner, Ellis and Andrea'r gonna take you for the grand tour and introduce you to Tines. He'll wanna meet you."

Ellis's face was the most expressionless of them all. He didn't emote when John said his name. Instead, he opened his jaw and poured tan sauce into the back of his throat straight from the antique gravy boat. The still-steaming gel leaked down his angular chin. He stared lifelessly at Janice, masticating an almost inhuman mouthful of food with vigor.

Janice felt sick.

"Eat up. One rule'a this house is you ain't leaving this table til you've eaten." John grinned over his hunk of meat. Grease rivulets danced around his veiny wrists.

Janice obeyed, timidly forking the smallest steak onto the ornate stargazer lily design on her porcelain plate, stuffing down her disgust. She sliced off a sliver and placed it on her tongue. It erupted with flavor, unlike anything she'd ever eaten. Seasoned to perfection, though a bit raw and stringy for her taste. The aroma steaming up into her face made her stomach howl out like a wild, starving dog for more. She started sawing off larger hunks until she, too, was stuffing her youthful face with reckless abandon. She forked over a half ear of corn next and dug her teeth into the hot, buttery kernels, exploding like delicious mini fireworks.

Janice hadn't had a proper meal like this in ages, and though the sickly bunch seemed nauseating to her, she was suddenly awash with the soothing sense of familial community she'd been plunged into forcefully with her distant relatives.

***

After gorging on the lavish feast, Ellis and Andrea Mitchell started the tour, as promised. Ellis led the girls through the yard at a leisurely pace, as was his unhurried nature for just about everything except eating. Janice, carefully observed her surroundings. Andrea trailed, slower still, from the rear.

As the teens made their way through the yard toward the dirt road perforating a staunch divide between the house and crops, Janice could tell that Ellis's gait wasn't quite right. The sixteen-year-old staggered and limped on seemingly wobbly legs. He ran both fists up the straps of his jean bibs, ones like his Father's but not quite as filthy. His arms sported dozens of healed, deep scars made with straight implements like an animal tangled in razor wire unfortunate enough to survive.

Andrea had similar cuts, too, scattered across exposed limbs among a deep and vibrant constellation of bruises. Janice wondered if Uncle John had some sordid history of child abuse. She feared Lynn might have pawned her off on some violent maniac. The kids and Marsha hadn't appeared fearful or skittish around him at dinner, though it was hardly enough time to judge.

Maybe they mutilated each other, Janice pondered. It certainly wouldn't be the first brutal sibling rivalry of Cain and Abel proportions.

"I can't wait to show you the hole." A smile wriggled on Ellis' color-drained face, his cloudy eyes unblinking. He limped a crooked path back and forth playfully through precise, parallel rows of sugar beets that stretched on beyond a full acre.

Janice examined the robust crops, foliage vibrant and plump. An acre of lush golden wheat grew on each side of the sugar beets, and at least another acre beyond sprawled two more acres of tall, shamrock green corn stalks flowing in the wild Wyoming wind like angry, churning ocean waves.

Beyond the corn sat a flat parcel of bare dirt. Further still were two side-by-side massive barns looming in the darkened sky with a cow pasture on one side and a towering grain silo on the other, protruding from the earth like a snuffed cigarette butt stabbed cherry-first into an ashtray.

Janice imagined the freedom of growing up with that much land. Back in the city, the kids had no real front yard, and the backyard was packed with clutter from Lynn's disgusting post-divorce hoarding spell. Janice would be hard-pressed to find a place to simply lay down a towel if she wanted to sunbathe.

The Mitchell kids, however, had miles of land on which to run amok. Janice couldn't even see the next farm due to the massive property. She could be isolated just about anywhere out here if she wanted to be alone with her thoughts.

They bee-lined to the cornfield, stomping fresh, reckless paths. The Mitchells darted around, quickening their paces through the seven-foot hissing stalks. Janice found herself struggling to keep up. In the epicenter of the dense throng of foliage, she'd completely lost track of them. Through the thick cloud cover, an overhead bark of thunder made her cower, reverting her instantly to a defenseless child. Despite knowing she wouldn't be lost for long in just over an acre, Janice still found herself in this strange world and became overwrought with claustrophobic panic.

"Andrea?" Janice screamed, dodging the slapping green hands of abusive vegetation. She rushed onward, catching a glimpse of something moving through the dim evening air, thick with humidity from the impending storm. It was Ellis' blonde hair bobbing awkwardly like an odd bouncy ball through the plants. Janice picked up speed and tripped over a thick tangle of broom-like tendrils of plant root. She dropped like a rock.

Beneath her, something extraordinary happened:

The ground moved.

Soil writhed under her palms. It was like a copper-scented, tumultuous sea of dirt. Fear choked her throat as if by a strangling hand. She was too terrified to move. She couldn't comprehend what she was palpating in the arid soil. Underneath the crumbling dirt, the ground was alive. Thousands upon thousands of worms squished and squirmed in a tangled plane of spaghetti just an inch or two below average-looking ground. Janice hadn't noticed it before, but from her hands and knees, she could see it well: the corn plants were moving. They flowed not just top-side with the wind from the rushing storm but also with the flourishing organic activity beneath their roots. It reminded her of psychedelic 'shrooms she'd partaken in just last year with a boyishly handsome emo senior she'd been trying to impress. Corn stalks pulsed and swayed for her now, just as the earth had back then.

Janice clenched her fingers, too entranced to scream. To confirm it wasn't a delusion, she sunk them down into the soil like a fleshy fork. She felt the slick throng of tiny worms slinking around against one another, creating one huge mass like a gigantic wad of distressed intestines. Guts shuddering with displeasure beneath the topsoil. Several organisms latched on her hand like thin, translucent leeches. She shook them off, eyes bulging, and plucked up just one for closer examination.

It wasn't a normal earthworm. It was smaller, thinner, and the end split off into three heads like some sort of squirming trident, translucent and milky. The tiny insect was vastly different from anything she'd ever seen in junior-level biology.

Their heads weren't round either. They were pointy, each punctuated with a tiny set of jelly-pink jaws. Their gaping, hungry, hinged mouths clamped shut and shot back open, all three out of sync. She whipped the creature away in utter disgust, clamored back to her feet, and smacked the worms from her knees and hands. Screaming shrilly, she blasted through the corn, heart banging in her chest and blood pressure pounding, forcing her head to throb violently.

Outside the field, Janice soon found her cousins. They were stopped. Still. They were on their knees, staring at a hole between them and a burgundy barn full of cattle. Their clouded eyes were huge, still unblinking. The ground around the hole looked like Uncle John had doused it with a five-gallon bucket of rust-colored paint. It smelled like something once living was in the summer heat, actively rotting. An audible swarm of flies accompanied the wretched stench, swarming in a black swirl around the orifice in the ground like minuscule buzzards.

"Guys, you'll never believe what I just saw!" Janice laughed, an inappropriate response to the surging terror.

She peered down over the opening to examine what the other two were so enamored with.

It was just a hole. A perfect three-inch diameter tube straight down into the earth like a plumbing pipe.

Ellis bent forward and placed his hands flat on the stinking muddy dirt around the opening. He closed his savage little eyes. It was the first time Janice remembered seeing any of them blink.

"Tines," he said, voice reverent, "this is Janice, our cousin. She's blood kin to us, Lord.

We pray you like her." He tilted his head to the side and pressed his bare ear against the mucky cavity. Two hungry flies and a crazed grin crept across his young face. "Yes, Lord, she's eaten from your harvest." After a pause, he nodded at the response from the hole, sending both flies back into the buzzing swarm.

Silence.

Janice remembered Ellis being a devout Christian last she knew, so hearing him speak to the perforation in the earth, referring to its contents as Lord, chilled her to the bone.

Andrea nudged Ellis aside. "Move! I want to hear Him!"

"Stop! Wait your turn, or He'll make Daddy feed you to him like Junior!"

Despite the silly sibling rivalry, the last few words Ellis uttered showered Janice in ice water.

"Wait, what did you just say?"

"Ugh." Ellis sighed as if he'd told the story a hundred times already. He sat up, dripping the reddened mud stamped on the side of his face like a traumatic head wound. Andrea scrambled to take his place, jamming her naked ear against the filthy opening. "We aren't supposed to talk about it with outsiders. They don't understand."

"Try me!" Janice ordered, her tone threatening. She slowly lowered to her knees toward the boy, acutely more aware of the dirt than ever.

They were squirming again, wriggling as a unified squishy mass beneath the powdery surface of the land. She cringed and bolted back upright immediately. She could still feel them swelling beneath her feet.

"Do you feel that?" Janice motioned down at the ground, and Ellis became overjoyed.

"You already feel them?" Excitement coursed through his tone, his nebulous eyes still smoggy and dazed. "You really are a Mitchell, alright!"

Andrea started speaking to the gash in the soil again. "Gladly, Lord! You must be starving!" Andrea held a scarred, battered hand open. "Gimme the knife, Ellis! Tines wants some!"

Wants what?

Janice was afraid to ask aloud.

Ellis handed Andrea a folding knife from the front chest pocket of his bibs, and Janice stared with wild fascination. Andrea flipped out the blade and, with its half-serrated edge, sawed it against the side of her forearm, gnawing into her own peaky flesh. She dropped her arm down, hovering her fingers just inches over the opening in the earth. Squiggling lines of blood clung to her dirty skin and fanned out on the back of her tendonous hand like Merlot-colored corn roots, dripping down the hole.

"Watch this, Janice! You're not going to believe this!" Ellis rubbed his frail mitts together rapidly and stared back across the farm from which they'd traveled.

Suddenly, Andrea and Ellis erupted in celebratory jumps and cheerful gasps.

Janice studied the landscape, but nothing was different about the expanse of land before them.

Nothing had changed.

"Wow! Look at him go," Ellis exclaimed, pointing to the wheat field.

Both of Janice's cousins' eyes trailed simultaneously as if they were witnessing the same events in tandem.

Andrea bounced joyfully, flinging droplets of blood on the dirt as she clapped. Her typically uninterested voice was bursting with life now. "It's such an honor to be in His presence!"

They were witnessing something wonderful.

"What am I missing?" Janice hollered, frustrated. "I don't see anything."

Andrea yelled loudly over her shoulder through the quiet, humid air, as if hollering over the music in a deafening nightclub. "It took us a while to see it, too, but once you do, it's incredible!"

Janice tensed. The cousins continued to rejoice, demented eyes flitting maniacally in sync with some imaginary entity, both experiencing a bizarre group hallucination as they ruffled through wheat and galloped blissfully over sugar beets. From across the field, John and Marsha bound out of the door to their farm, beholding the same invisible presence the kids were.

But the adults weren't jovial.

John dropped to his knees and emitted a guttural, weepy howl Janice could hear from across the farm, though faint. Marsha wrapped her arms around him as an act of comfort. Janice had only seen Uncle John cry once in her entire life:

At Junior's funeral.

Janice leaned against an out-of-commission combine and tried to make sense of the lunacy she was witnessing. Anxiety swirled in her mind, constricting her chest and blackening her vision. She backed up against the barn, afraid to go anywhere near the putrid, reeking hole. Afraid of Ellis and Andrea. Afraid that the woman who was supposed to protect her had instead dumped her off with four deviant, hallucinating fiends.

Her tennis shoe drug against something. Upon closer inspection, she realized the trip hazard was a sun-faded, dirt-encrusted plastic stegosaurus. Andrea plopped beside Janice, digging her bony fingers into the earth, tossing handfuls upward, and raining soil down lovingly on herself. Horror sloughed in the pit of her stomach as Janice witnessed a smattering of ghastly three-headed worms tangled in her cousin's hair.

"Isn't it amazing?" Andrea asked, joy sparkling across her slightly foggy irises. "Can you hear Tines' voice yet? It might be too soon. I didn't at first, either. Neither did Ellis. He spoke to Daddy first."

Janice stared at Andrea with eyes so bulged that they blurred the center of her vision. Ellis approached. Flanked from both sides. She wanted to run.

Where could she go? The next property had to be at least a mile or two away.

Ellis spoke, winded from frolicking. "Daddy heard the voices first. Before any of us. We thought he was crazy. We looked at him like you're looking at us now." His spirits had been so completely dampened earlier, yet now he was exuberant. "Then Tines, that's what we call Him," he pointed to the hole, "told Daddy that if he made a sacrifice to the land, the land would make a larger sacrifice to us. So, Junior... he had to go."

Andrea interrupted. "He's with Tines now. In the earth. Buried behind the pasture over there." She switched gears. "Daddy lured him out to the hole with a brand-new dinosaur toy."

"Junior loved dinosaurs," Ellis interrupted, manic.

"Then Daddy ran him over with the harrow." Andrea motioned at a blue tractor beside the barn.

Trailing behind was a hydraulic disc harrow with a row of eighteen-inch unyielding circular steel blades. The evenly spaced metal, once used for harvesting wheat crops, was coated with sprigs of blond hair and brown blood drier than the soil beneath the machine.

"Don't worry, he wasn't looking. Papa put him down real fast." Ellis tried to soothe her.

Janice thought she was going to be sick again.

"Daddy took it real hard. He didn't want to have to grind up Junior, not one bit. He loved Junior."

"Junior was his favorite," Andrea said, rolling her foggy eyes disdainfully.

"But the farm was failing, and he had to do something. For the good of the family," Ellis spouted factually.

"And Tines delivered," Andrea exclaimed. "When Daddy bought the farm, nothing would grow here. We kept having blight and standin' water and pests eatin' holes in the veggies. But once Junior was gone, Tines stuck those big metal spikes up through the earth and prepared all the dirt. He mixed in the blood and gave the soil all the minerals it needed."

"Now everything is lush and green. Crops grow like weeds now! This is the only farm that produces anything in miles," Ellis added.

Andrea held up her arm. "That's why we feed Tines a little here and there, so we don't have to give up another Junior."

The blood was beginning to encrust itself, hardening on her pale, scarred skin.

"I don't think Daddy could handle another sacrifice. Mom, neither."

Janice touched the toy dinosaur, hoping that the tactile texture of its plastic scales would keep her grounded through the insanity. She stared over the wheat and sugar beets at John, acres away, sobbing hard into Marsha's chest.

"Oh, Janice, soon you'll be able to see it all. Every time we feed him, he rips and shreds the ground so's that roots can grow strong. That's why the food is so delicious. It's Tines' way of givin' back!"

Janice's head swirled with the nonsensical notions they'd filled her head with. She turned her thoughts to the sea of squiggling life forms in the soil. With her back pressed to the barn, her heart thumped so fiercely it resonated through the splintered wood.

A Holstein cow poked its head over the rail and pressed his face to hers. The sudden surprise touch of the animal made her scream. She jolted, pushing away the cow's sinewy face. But something was strange about the animal. She examined it closer.

The bovine was as nauseating and sickly as the rest of the Mitchell family. Its skin stretched taut across its bones, boldly illustrating its structural anatomy. She caressed it, staring into its hazy irises. A trident-shaped worm wriggled its way out of the slick sclera and slithered its translucent body along the cow's murky cornea, biting its way across the squishy eyeball with its clamping rows of bristly teeth.

Janice thought about the origins of the steak she'd scarfed hungrily at dinner and threw up by the side of the barn, retching again every time she thought about the animal's wormy eyeball. She imagined the entire Mitchell family riddled with wriggling parasites, worms gnawing their way through spoiled vegetable-laden digestive tracts and squishing through hole-ridden strainer-like stomachs that seethed tainted beef through a maze of chewed wormholes.

Janice imagined her own body crawling with the maggoty creatures and pictured her nubile flesh pulsing with life other than her own, just like the ground she knelt on now.

She recalled a lecture she'd half-slept through months back about the effects of tapeworms on the human body and how things like toxoplasmosis cause delusions and schizophrenia because of the parasite's effects in a perfect-storm setting of the human cerebrum.

Janice slumped among the contaminated bovines, infested corn fields, wormy soil, and completely mad extended family, watching Ellis and Andrea frolic through the wheat like they were playing in Heaven's clouds.

She threw up again, thinking about how much meat and corn she'd recently consumed. As Janice wiped her mouth, she felt something strange, something smooth and moving like a twisting rubber band with ends grinding like sandpaper against the side of her tongue. She dug down around her molar and fished out another three-headed translucent worm and flung it in horror at the ground, letting out a blood-curdling scream. As it echoed through the miles of surrounding farmland, she knew that whatever these things were, they were now inside her, embedding themselves in a truly insidious way.

"I know it's scary, but I promise it'll all be better once He finally speaks to you."

Andrea wrapped Janice in her two bony arms in a loving embrace.

***

Summer left swiftly, replaced incrementally by harsh autumnal winds and crisp, biting temperatures. The corn and wheat had long been harvested, and Tines now drug his six-foot steel fingernails up through the crumbling dirt, pulverizing packed soil, forming perfect minced rows for which the Mitchells would soon sow lengthy rows of cabbage, carrots, and lettuce with their feeble, malnourished hands. Crawling through squirming tidal waves of dirt on bony knees to do so.

Janice stood listlessly above the blood-splattered hole, stuffed with a fresh mash of cattle guts and human blood. She stared blankly through a curly mop of black-rooted lavender hair. She focused her hazy irises on the spectacular sight of those gigantic metal tines gnashing their way through the fragmented ground.

Though it was uncomfortable to smile, easier instead to relax into the vast expanse of dismal darkness encroaching in her mind, she couldn't resist raising the corners of her lips, clinging to one last bit of humanity and humor.

From the hole, that ungodly hole, His voice arose.

Janice heard it now.

They all did.

Thick, sanguine liquid dripped down the knife tip from her freshly carved wrist, dripping into the blackened hole. Tines's diabolical voice wafted wickedly up past a decaying coppery bib of rotten fluids, rising through the three-inch round incision in the earth's surface and oozing up like subway steam into the clean mountain air, thanking her for her sacrifice.

DERAILED

A loud groan fills the scorching summer air. A low bass growl, like something demonic has awakened, hungry and furious.

Is it the texture of the road, I wonder, or maybe the tire? I just had them rotated.

I flick through FM stations filled with staticky, muddled half-song hybrids where rhythmic hip-hop bleeds over Cat Scratch Fever's twangy electric guitar riff. I whirl the knob, flipping through worship, lonesome country, and several upbeat Latino songs I can't understand a word of, eager for my arrival back in New England. Hour five behind the wheel. Time's dragging.

The convention was a waste, I think. Didn't even sell enough photos to cover the cost of the booth.

Surprise, surprise, another financial backslide.

The violent, angry snarling in the air persists. I flick off the radio to eliminate it as a suspect. It's not the source. I roll down my window, one with peeling UV coating. The ominous sound rages like something otherworldly.

It's the tire.

Something's very wrong. Anxiety nips at my stomach lining, and my breath catches in my chest. I've heard this before, long ago when my first vehicle, a raggedy junkyard-salvaged Taurus I'd rebuilt with my uncle, exploded a tire going 20 mph in a suburban neighborhood. Now I'm doing 80, sandwiched between travelers.

"Fuck." The word tumbles from my glossy lips.

The slow lane is packed like staggered bricks with barreling semi trucks, cruising almost bumper-to-bumper. I slap my turn signal and eye the treacherous height of the cliff on my left. The only thing separating us all from a murky pit below is a knee-high, stubby metal guardrail along the asphalt's edge. No shoulder. Just a perilous drop to the bottom.

My only option is the other side of the road… and fast.

Drivers forge on, oblivious to my frantic, oxidized blinker, weakly flickering in the scorching summer sun.

"C'mon, let me in—"

BANG!

A deafening sound fills the air as a rear tire blows. The SUV's steering becomes squirrelly. I try desperately not to panic.

Over-correcting is the worst thing you can do. At least, that's what Uncle Henry had always repeated growing up.

I decelerate, trying to keep the car straight. I'm packed between speeding vehicles like a sardine. The wheel trembles violently in my hand. A slight gap forms to my right, with bumpers parting like Moses with the Red Sea made of molasses. Now is my only chance to get to the shoulder.

The wheel below my white knuckles feels like it's going to jiggle out of the steering column. I veer right. The rest of the tire explodes like a bomb under me with a second loud bang. It whirls my SUV, whipping me perpendicularly from noon to three o'clock.

I connect my eyes with the oncoming semi-driver like a deer before it bursts into a bombed shell of ichor roadside. He careens toward me, unable to stop his barreling rig fast enough. I can see it in his eyes. Eyes as certain they're about to partake in the finality of death's icy homecoming as mine. His mouth is agape in pure horror.

He knows he's about to end my life.

In a slow-motion second, I feel something in my bones, in my gut. The realization taints my meat with fear: This is it. This is where my life ends.

My blood turns to poison at the thought of blinking out of existence in three… two…

The force from the tire's secondary and more severe explosion slingshots my SUV off the cliff at breakneck speed. There's no guardrail to slow me down. Just a wide shoulder that I careen off. The fleeting relief from a narrow escape with the semi gives way to a worse looming fate. As I fly off the side of the road, the back of the vehicle slams against the craggy edge of the pavement and, by pure unfortunate chance, flips me upside down. I'm a kamikaze bird, dive bombing. Powerless. Weightless.

No, I correct myself the second before the impact: THIS is where I die.

The inverted g comes at me like an abusive fist to the face. I smash with full chaotic power into the ditch like I'm hitting a brick wall with all my energy. Too hard to survive.

Smash!

The car accordions into a low spot in the ditch. Hundreds of pounds of metal and glass smash the unyielding soil with brutal force and speed.

It's the loudest sound I've ever heard or will ever hear again. Blue glass shatters, blowing across my face like painful angel kisses, forming a sparkling sea above, which my shaken brain knows… should be below. Toothy shards twinkle overhead like a glimmering art installation in a gallery of powdery loam. I reach for it, and my battered fingertips graze them. I'm grabbing for anything. The fragments clink like an ethereal wind chime.

My face is wet. I cannot see out of my right eye. And somehow, that's still the least of my worries.

A noose holds me upside down. I'm strangled by the smooth belt clasped at the waist buckle like some death sentence prisoner who didn't get to have her last words. Pain courses into my throbbing skull in glugs like an emptying jug, pooling behind my straining, soaked face.

I try to scream. The strap squelches the cry in my throat. The crushed roof cradles my swelling skull like a pair of skeletal hands. My chin is almost fused to my sternum at an unnatural angle, clamping my jaw like a vice, my molars embedded in the flesh of my tongue. I wonder if my neck is broken, but it's all a moot point if I suffocate to death.

The engine block scorches the skin of my shattered leg, obscured by the cracked dashboard. Thrashing with every fiber of my being, I growl through my gritted teeth, slobbering a pathetic, terrified, muffled plea for help.

The car is quiet except for the sound of my liquefied grunts, the floundering of my pinned torso, and the whizzing of cars traveling on the highway.

My vision grows dark, and that's when the real trouble begins.

***

Mom's house hasn't changed at all in the decade I've avoided it like the plague. The sickly concoction of herbal remedies dirties the humid air hanging thick in my nostrils. It's familiar and noxious. It took years to rid the smell. All of my clothes had to be tossed. The fibers clung to the offensive odor of those awful days. I'd catch a whiff and tumble against every pothole and divot down this twisted memory lane.

I've worked for years to escape her clutches, ushering my little sister out the door before making a grand middle-finger exit myself, and in some cruel twist of fate, I'm back here again, peering at her aging face, rife with stress furrows and frown lines through the only eye I have left.

She apologizes for the broken swamp cooler unit in the window, the ancient one that's been there since I was a teenager. The one fused to the siding with caked grime and an annual deluge of bird shit. She explains the rats gnawed the wiring. Her tone is quiet and conspiratorial, and more than anything, her seriousness is unnerving.

She adds, "But what's new? They think they can rattle me, but they have another thing coming. I've got God and belemnite on my side." She caresses the fossil on her homemade necklace. It looks like a rifle shell made of stone with a string through it. On par with all of her jewelry, it's hideous.

I find humor in Mom thinking vermin are trying to run her out. I lived with her for twenty years, and I can say that I pity the rodents. They should get out while they still can.

With one gravelly statement out of her mouth, I'm flooded with a recollection of everything I hate about her. Over the last thirty years, I've gotten a front-row ticket to her loony-bin talent show. I've watched a handful of unmedicated mental illnesses methodically erode the normalcy of her once June Cleaver-like existence, morphing her into this strange paranoia-riddled zealot who has apparently only continued down her winding path since I left.

She helps me up to my crutches and feels my forehead with her perspiration-drenched palm. The broken unit converts the room into a sauna in the midday Florida heat. She studies the sweat and wipes it on her blue jeans. I'd wager a bet they haven't been washed in at least two months.

She smiles at me, a hopeful one, and says, "I'm so glad you're home."

The sentiment makes me want to vomit after all we've been through. After the unhealthy conditions and the animosity. After the fear, chaos, and confusion she'd subjected us to for decades. This house was never a home.

It's a prison where two children were held hostage for decades against their will.

*＊＊

Mom is crawling on the narrow strip of the crumb-and-grime-covered carpet she's unearthed. Seeing the disheveled condition of this cluttered mess makes my stomach flip. This house should have been condemned by the state long ago. She's masked the windows with rolls of stick-on vinyl in the design of expensive stained glass, but the cuts aren't precise, and the gaps look tacky from afar. But they've served their purpose of forcing privacy from passers-by, so she deems them 'money well spent.'

Stacks of unread magazines and self-help books are piled upon broken fax machines, digital cameras, laptop paperweights, and old corded telephones: all things she hasn't had a use for in ages. Everything is heaped in haphazard piles, some chest high, many shrouded by cloth, their heaped contents unknown.

When I try to take in the whole living room at once, it looks like a chaotic magic eye, but without the use of both of mine, I fail to see the answer hidden beneath. At the far wall, I see a few inches of white leather peeking out from massive hoards of miscellaneous items and want to laugh. I guess there is still a couch here, after all.

"What are you doing?" I ask. But I don't know why I ask. The response isn't going to be normal. It isn't going to be: I dropped my earring and I'm looking for it.

"Eavesdropping on the O.R.," she whispers, swinging her head back so I can see she's using a filthy doctor's stethoscope.

There it is.

There's the crazy.

Behind her, I notice several baited snap-traps, their jaws open, ready to clamp down on soft fur. She presses the circular end of the scope back to the carpet, and I wish more than anything I could stop the stupid fucking words from sliding out of my busted lips as I ask, "What's the O.R.?"

I hate myself for engaging in her lunacy. I hate myself for being so nonchalant and unsurprised.

More than anything, I hate that this is normal.

"Order of the Rodentia. Didn't you get all those pamphlets I sent you?" She holds the stethoscope back to the floor and moves it to the wall, uninterested in my answer. "It's going to be dark soon. At about five p.m., they have their first meeting of the evening, where they strategize. If I don't get a belemnite puck placed near enough—"

"That's alright. You... do your thing." I wave her off, struggling to pass through the narrow labyrinth of junk into the kitchen.

My stomach grumbles, and I can't think of a single proper meal I've had since the accident. Just hospital jello and some sort of meat slab they called Salisbury steak. The lie detector determined that that was a lie.

The ceiling in the kitchen is still blackened by the great cooking disaster of 1996, the one where mom left tortellini noodles boiling on high heat with a plastic spoon still in the pot years ago. She started the food, forgot promptly, and left the house for a while. My sister and I smelled smoke hours later and emerged to an obsidian cloud, raging fire licking the wall behind the stove. With the house itself being a giant tinderbox, a hazard even back then, we thought quickly. I put out the flames with a sink sprayer on high, and Sis shook a two-liter of diet soda from the fridge at it. We tackled it like amateur child firefighters with surprising success.

Mom was unfazed when she returned. Almost a little delighted. She didn't apologize. The crisis gave her an excuse to spend two days shopping for a 'good deal on a hotplate.' We never used the hotplate much. Mostly ended up eating fast food dollar menu items or delivery for the next few years...

Ahh, memories.

Twelve years later, here I am, staring at a used thrift store hotplate on top of a nonworking stove against a still-blackened wall. Welcome home.

I decide I'll order pizza.

Just like old times.

***

My broken phone chimes and the cracked screen floods with light. I open it to see a text from Dildo saying, "What up, hoochie mama? Still have any teeth left?"

I reply, "No. But I hear gummy blowjobs are all the rage, so Imma start charging double when I get back on them streets."

"Don't forget my 30% cut, ho."

"Don't worry. I won't."

"How's the monster?"

I text her a quote from a book I read aloud to her as a child. One of my favorite bits from Homer's Odyssey: "Still waiting there in your halls, poor woman, suffering so, her life an endless hardship."

"Classic." After a moment, another chime. "Arrrg, matey, send pics of 'yer eyepatch, Cap'n Sparrow."

I snap a crappy selfie of me flipping her the bird, nude-colored patch in full view. I reply again. "How's the trip, bitch?"

"Lame. My flight back is on Monday. I'll come save you right after I land."

"You're my she-ro."

I miss her.

"Has mom made you wear a belemnite necklace yet to ward away the secret cabal of mouse-people?"

"We are called the Order of Rodentia, thank you very much. I can't wear it. It'll burn my skin."

I laugh a little at our silly back-and-forth. I send another message. "I've infiltrated the nest. Gathering intel. I'll report back at 14:00 hours tomorrow with my findings."

Mom interrupts my text with a soft knuckle rap on the door. I lob my cell on the comforter. The smell of sizzling mushrooms and garlic mixes with her herbal stink in the air, and my senses shift like a volatile roller coaster.

"Food's here." Her voice is quiet as she hands it off to me. She looks down at my phone to steal a glance at my conversation. I don't care enough to cover it up. She already knows I'm certain she's crazy. After a pause, she adds, "Please, whatever you do, don't leave any food out. You know, for the—"

"For the O.R.?" I cut her off. I don't think my pizza crumbs will make any difference in their population, which, due to the filth throughout the house, is, I'm sure, admittedly enormous.

She's got her victimized face on now. The one she flashes in public often. The one that works, time and again. And, despite my knowing it's a mask she wears when it's convenient for her to get comfort and attention, my inner, kinder human blurts out something to smooth things over. To spare us both the poor me, everyone hates me look.

"Want a piece?"

"Sure," she says, forcing a weak, dejected smile. I doubt she's had anything to eat other than the grocery checkout bag of gumballs and a two-liter of diet cola she chugged straight out of the bottle at lunchtime today. I'm astonished she's made it this far in life with her beyond-questionable life choices.

Before Dad left, he used to stare at her from afar through the sides of his narrowed eyes and mutter about how she'll outlive us all one day, surviving on pure spite. Unfortunately, he's probably right.

I offer up the box, and she holds up a finger full of cheap, chintzy costume jewelry rings piled atop each other like she's had some sudden epiphany and scurries off. I hold up the cooling pie, rolling my remaining eye as things clatter in the kitchen. I hear boxes shifting and plastic spice containers falling, followed by a whispered Goddammit.

She returns with an old shaker that used to contain Italian seasoning and says theatrically, with way too much pep, "I know you like it with parm!" She wings her hands out and widens her excited expression like she's auditioning for the role of Roxie Hart on Broadway.

I smile. Her efforts, however misguided, seem kind of sweet as she shakes off-white fluff on all but one piece. She takes the bare slice and bows like I'm royalty, which I suppose would be weird for another parent, but is right on-brand with her quirky extra-ness, and she backs toward the door.

Despite preferring time alone, I invite her to join me.

It's the humane thing to do.

She says she can't and mumbles something about having 'much work to do yet.' Something about how rodentia outnumber us eight-to-one and sleep in shifts to study human behavior 24/7. She yammers something crazy about a theory she's got and I catch words like "Trojan horse" and "Troy" and "Homer's Odyssey" and "Taking them apart to see the recording devices inside."

I pretend to listen, bobbing my head and saying "Mmmmm-hmmmmm" and "Oh, wow" on a loop every 4-7 seconds and thinking about how strange it is she just mentioned the Odyssey too and how delicious this pizza is compared to hospital food, wishing she hadn't dusted it in that expired stale-tasting crap.

There's something sad in her eyes when she realizes I'm not listening. Not her typical charade where she pretends to be melancholy, on the verge of shedding crocodile tears that might as well be oil or gelatin.

No, it's a genuinely lonely look.

At this moment, she looks small and pitiful, and I feel ashamed. Sorry, I've grown this intolerant of her. Sorrier still, that I'd rather be anywhere in the world but here. I'm still counting down the minutes until my sister's plane lands and I can leave this cursed dump.

She shuffles out the door, defeated, and I shovel slices down carefully, my tongue fat and tender where my molars sliced right through during the crash.

As I polish off the box, I think about what kind of employers and potential men in the dating pool are going to desire a one-eyed, emotionally constipated thirty-something photographer with a shattered tibia and mommy issues.

I'm sure both are gonna be real winners.

***

Screaming, I wake from an image of me behind the wheel, watching upside-down grass come at me at breakneck speed. My eye shoots open the moment I smash into the ground and taste too-real dirt on my tongue.

But it's not soil I am tasting after all. A hefty, brown rat's long hind feet skitter across my face, and I taste the bristly fur of its finely segmented tail as it curls into my mouth and slaps my tongue. I whack reflexively at it. It smashes into the headboard and slinks off into a mound of clutter, making the mound writhe and pulse beneath it as if the house is alive. As if mom's hoarded junk has a living, breathing life of its own.

Though the paranoid cult talk is ridiculous, Mom is right about one thing. Humans are outnumbered by the vermin in this house.

Unnerved, my heart racing, I cringe and gag. I hobble my bruised body to my crutches and clunk my way into the bathroom down the hall, knocking a pile of dusty recipe books over on my way in. I am not picking those up.

I lather my toothbrush and scrub traces of rodent from my tongue, wanting to hurl every time I remember it. I pee, and before I flush, I notice the bowl is full of blood. I think about what day it is.

The fifth.

It's nowhere near that time of the month.

The contents of the toilet are alarming. I wonder if there's some internal damage from the accident the doctor didn't catch. Perforated kidney or something. I look at my abdomen, which is a mess of bruises, markedly worse than yesterday, which is strange. I spit the paste and rinse my brush, but the dingy, cracked bowl of the sink looks like a crimson Jackson Pollock painting, too. I bare my teeth in the grime-flecked mirror, expecting to see torn stitches. Instead, my gums are bleeding, gushing to refill the crevices after every mouthful I expel.

I examine my face, rife with sliced stripes from shattered safety glass, and see the maroon strip of skin where my seat belt held me like the Boston Strangler's choke-hold. The term damaged goods comes to mind as I take in my image as a complete package.

My pained stomach gurgles and I feel like I am about to shit my pajama shorts.

What the hell is happening? One blown tire and my life unravels at the seams. My life has derailed.

I stare into the mirror as sanguine drool dribbles from my lips, and I flashback to a glimpse I caught of myself in my rear-view before I blacked out days ago. Tendrils of ruby liquid from an almost-severed tongue and ocular fluid from the emptying socket in my face trickled up my injured cheeks to my vein-popped forehead.

"Mom!" I yell, like I'm a lost child in a department store again, five years old, trying to echo-locate her by the jingling jailer-style cluster of keys she wore on a ring around her wrist to distract people's gaze from the scarred slashes underneath.

I stumble, dizzy, down the hallway toward her living room, though the only living done in there was not an aspirational kind. It should be called an existing room.

I lean on a precarious mass of clutter as tall as me, covered in a dingy bed sheet as if the soiled cloth were some invisibility cloak. The haphazard pile topples over, and we both crash down. I tumble through the junk like a pinball through the chaotic landscape onto a narrow stripe of dirty, threadbare carpet that reeks of years-old dog piss. It's now stamped with my seeping vermilion saliva. I groan as my crutches clatter against my bruised torso. One smacks the knot on the back of my head. Reaching out to grab onto something to right myself, my fingers make an unforeseen mistake.

SNAP!

The sound rings out. I realize instantly what it is. The sound bites through the air like a gnashing set of angry teeth again, and searing pain shoots through the one bare foot, not in a cast. I feel one of my toes fracture instantly.

SNAP!

SNAP!

Now, one has clamped my hair and my ear together in a tangled mess. Unforgiving rat traps clamp against my flesh like stinging little vices.

"Mom!"

I'm bawling now like a chickenshit baby who just wants her mommy. The pain in my extremities is acute, but the wrenching and throbbing in my abdomen is far worse.

I wretch blood onto the carpet. Too much.

I am beyond alarmed. I am terrified again. As terrified as I was careening off the embankment. Catching the eyes of the semi-driver. Feeling the life being choked out of me. Light-headed. I can't get the traps off. I'm blinded by my own tears, and the mat of hair tangled over my only remaining eye.

She's here.

I feel her blurred form in my liquid periphery, melding with the junk piles dressed like ghosts in sheets. She lowers to me, and my fear spreads. Her face is not furrowed with concern.

No.

She's pleased.

There's something in her hand, something glinting in the dim light beaming in through dingy curtains and the faux stained glass pattern. She attempts to wipe the hair from my face, but it only tangles further in the snap trap snarled in my locks. She places a knee on either side of me and presses her body onto my distended abdomen.

I burp more blood onto myself. There's foam in it, creating pink ocean waves, lapping across my face like the nearby coastal tides. Her weight feels like it's crushing me, and I can't breathe.

Smothered again, this time by the thighs of my mother like some reverse birthing ceremony.

Blinded again, this time by my own frothy gastric juices instead of windshield glass.

Choking again, but this time on words that won't come out. That can't come out.

"Sent like the Trojan horse right to my doorstep. You are a clever breed, aren't you?"

Her voice is calm. Eerie.

I am afraid to flail for fear I'll find more obscured snap traps the hard way. I writhe, struggling beneath her burdensome weight. I see the bestrewn kitchen through the war-torn battlefield of my childhood home.

I see the landline on the wall, cord gnawed through by sharpened front teeth, frayed, dialing outgoing calls only to purgatory. Beside it, my spent pizza box, the makeshift Parmesan canister, and an opened container of rat poison. On it, a colorful cartoon rat with two Xs for eyes.

He looks like I feel. My ocular cavity is nothing more than a withered cavern with a pirate patch, and, like him, I hear death's beckoning whisper in my ear.

"I knew something was up when you refused to touch the belemnite. That was my first clue. Then, last night, I caught you red-handed. Communicating with the others. Providing intel for your leader. You sick piece of shit. I don't know what you've done to my daughter, but you did a damn fine job on this Trojan horse clone. Looks just like her."

She smiles and holds up the knife in her hand. My stinging eye bulges at the sight of its sharpened edge as she twirls it over me.

"She hadn't called in years. Now, she suddenly needed to be taken in? Well, you may have infiltrated Troy, but you will never win this war! Poison is what the rat deserves."

I gasp for air as her blade presses into the maltreated flesh near my collarbone, burying the thin metal deeper and deeper as white-hot pain shoots through me in waves. I slap at her, nailing her in the face with the small wooden plank smashed to my purple fingers, but it doesn't phase her. She's looking at me like she doesn't even recognize me. Like I'm some nefarious impostor.

I scream with everything in me.

She shoves the knife downward until the tip pierces bone. She removes it and slices again. Stabbing into my abdomen until the hilt touches my rib. My dulling, toxic malaise mixes with the sharp agony of the cuts.

I feel her prodding inside of me with the blade, like some curious kid with a dissected frog in science class. In this final slow-motion second, I think about how she will find nothing inside of me but bones ceasing to provide protection. Arteries slowing their pumps. Mangled connective tissue no longer connecting. Synapses like wet fireworks, failing to fire. Vital organs no longer vital.

I know now that I was wrong to think it, crushed inside my vehicle last week. This is it. This is where my life ends. As full circle as anything could ever be in this world.

She brought me into it. Now she is taking me out.

As darkness descends like a black velvet curtain at the end of some twisted final act, I hear my mother as she prods my innards and squints, searching curiously for wires, cables, circuit boards, and cameras hidden within me, buried deep within my abused flesh. Her voice is like some sick lullaby, sung to her firstborn child one final time. She looks at me like she's about to solder the circuit board of a VCR and says, "Let's see what kind of technology you've got in there. Tell me, what makes you tick, you little fucking rat?"

PAINTED IN VERMILION

Duncan trembled on the seat near the bay window, which provided an all-too-vivid panorama of the carnage. For the first time, maybe ever, he yearned for his mother's embrace.

Like the blustery winter air shredding through the darkened night sky, she no longer offered warmth or comfort. Her selfish heart had never really been capable of much beyond narcissism. She often fed, much like those things, on attention garnered through self-sabotage, wallowing in misery, feasting hungrily on the empathy of anyone sympathetic enough to entertain her constant gush of one-sided tales of woe.

Now, her rotund body was slumped limply upright, seated against the whistling fireplace. The numbing December air oozed down the chimney flue, hardening her once-malleable body with rigor. Duncan avoided Tanya's glassy gaze and chilling stillness, focusing instead on the blood-spattered bricks near her foam-seething forehead.

The creatures inside her brain chittered, churning pulpy matter out of the opening in her skull. They burrowed deeper, in search of a warm spot in her ichor to implant their larvae. If she was anything like the others, soon her cavities would be birth canals to countless more, squirming together as an army, puppeteering her from within as one solitary twitching mass.

The swarm, operating as one bloodthirsty family, was similar in both form and ravenous appetite.

"They came in with the wind," Randall muttered soberly, staring out the kitchen window in horror.

It was all he could think to say in such a bleak moment, and every syllable was seeped in quiet terror. A vermilion insect hopped hard, its brutal-looking feet embedding razor-fine points into the glass near the enlarged, flitting eyes of his reflection, war-torn and angular.

Though surprisingly soft-spoken, Randall Bryant, having ended his last stint in the Army as a decorated drill sergeant, rarely expressed fear.

And never around the boy.

Duncan's eyes were transfixed, pleading wordlessly for guidance. A hundred machine-gunned questions impregnated the painful silence, none of which Randall had the answers for. A few houses down, a woman gushed forth a bloodcurdling scream.

He chewed his bottom lip. "Sounded like Mrs. Green."

The sleepy town teemed with panic, bustling with plague-like pandemonium. The crisp Connecticut air and frozen piles of windswept leaf litter brimmed with six-legged, four-winged organisms.

All red.

All hungry.

It was clear that the quaint tree-lined roads of rural Kent no longer belonged to the residents.

BANG, BANG, BANG!

A fist hammered against the thin glass behind Randall. He emitted a brief, undeniable yelp, something he hadn't done in years. Not since he was just a boy of eighteen chucked headfirst into the world of shelled hellscapes, echoing gunfire and deadly combat.

The explosive sound sent Randall into a flashback of the unintentional death of a Middle Easterner, some twelve or so years prior, while driving a candy delivery van. The civilian's face had been blown off by an IUD during Randall's second week in Afghanistan, and he'd been unlucky enough to witness firsthand the man's sudden decimation.

His face had been found, minutes later, haphazardly nestled in the rubble, like some carelessly discarded latex Halloween mask. Intact. Just a three-holed flap of skin. No skull or body in the vicinity.

Randall had taken a photo with his phone, astounded that such a feat was possible outside of the movies.

Even when the flood of memories faded, the smell of burning confections still permeated his senses. The scent of sugar had filled his throat with bile since that day. And when the IUD exploded all those years ago, baby-faced young Randall Bryant had made the exact same embarrassing yelp as now.

"I know you're in there, Bryant," a man barked, seething with aggression and distress. "Your truck's in the driveway!"

Randall composed himself, smoothing the hem of his gray t-shirt to the trembling, toned abdomen behind it.

"Let me in! It's not safe out here, and my place is crawling!" Fury melted to remorse. "They… They got 'em. Candace, Leena… My family's gone, Bryant. I'm…" His voice. "I'm the only one left."

The voice was Jack McKellan's, Randall's former neighbor and drinking buddy from a darker time before he'd discovered the balanced cycle of AA meetings and therapy that kept his aggression at bay. He hadn't heard Jack's voice in years, only tossed an occasional 'howdy' hand signal while scooping his son up for court-mandated weekends.

As he contemplated the consequences of opening the door, Randall gawked at Tanya, her brain churning, eyes wriggling back and forth by the roiling orgy of minuscule legs and darting wings and eyes burrowing in the balmy depths of her undulating skull.

"I don't think so, McKellan."

Randall's tone was stern, but there was an unnatural softness about him. Duncan feared that someone would eventually push his father over the edge, and they'd all witness the day Randall's faux passive nature inevitably gave way to intense violence.

He'd seen Tanya force Randall to the brink a few times before the divorce, often foolishly cornering him. She'd jam her index finger in his pectoralis like some infuriating, bottle-blonde woodpecker and squawk about his emotional deficiencies and how he'd failed to satisfy her ever-growing list of demands.

Duncan had been relieved when the two fully divorced. He'd been certain that if they'd stayed together, Tanya would end up…

Well, she would end up the same as she was now, he supposed.

Lifeless.

Drained.

An empty shell.

"Goddammit, Randy, you're really gonna leave me out here to die?!"

The man sobbed hard, but it wasn't an act. Both Randall and Duncan were all too familiar with Tanya's constant emotional manipulation and could discern crocodile tears.

Randall calculated all options, deciding succinctly. "Meet me by the kitchen door."

A muffled chuckle of relief filled the night air, bouncing merrily across the sound-dampening fluff powdered across the backyard.

"But, sir!" Duncan protested as his betrayed eyes bulged.

Randall quietly growled. "What did I teach you? Never leave a man behind."

Duncan scampered to the foyer, taking shelter among the hung coats and disorganized assortment of winter boots. He dropped to the floor and tucked himself into a nook between a heap of chopped firewood and the small hatchet used to cleave it.

In a flash, Jack scrambled inside and stomped off the accumulated snow. He winced and bent down to eye Tanya's gruesome head wound, examining the stirring beneath the gash in her cranium. His disgust melded with intrigue as he watched her remains undulate from the burrowing and squirming.

"Oh God... Tanya?"

Randall could see Jack's deep-set eyes were swollen and red, buried below two thick, black brows. A trail of snot and tears ran down to his chapped, colorless lips in glassy, converged streams.

"You... we...should get her outta here! Those things..." Jack soaked up the solemn vibe of the room and maneuvered mid-sentence to one of more reverence. "Sorry for your loss, Duncan."

Randall sighed. "You're right. I just," he paused, "I haven't wanted to touch her."

Jack flashed a wide-eyed, 'yeah-I-hear-that' glance and then moved toward the seated corpse. Both men grabbed the chirruping cadaver, her roiling flesh alive in a startling way. They dragged her across the grubby carpet and out the front door.

Duncan was relieved to break the appalling spell of his mother's remains. He listened to the men clamor and strain as they ejected Tanya from his childhood home and abandoned her roadside like carrion for the hungry crimson scavengers to feed on.

Duncan heard Jack holler, followed by both adults clattering back up the porch.

"Randall! Randall! What the HELL is that?!"

"Oh my God—"

"Randall?!"

Duncan clamored for a better view of the obscured battle but could only hear the men struggle as they fended someone — or something — off.

His father knew how to fight. It only happened under direct orders or when provoked, but the former soldier did have a tipping point. Duncan had seen it the night his parents split. The night he found his mother upended and screaming for the police in the bathroom after pecking Randall with that finger beak one too many times.

"Christ, where in the hell did that one even come from?"

"Oh God! Over there! By the Silverman place."

"What the...?" Jack's voice trailed.

Duncan's heart throbbed in his anxious chest. He mashed his face against the dining room window, seeking a voyeuristic glimpse, immediately awash with regret.

It was a swarm. Far too many to count. Thousands.

Possibly more.

Possibly lots more.

Silent, eerie, and astonishingly plentiful, they glinted beneath the streetlights. Hard, red exoskeletons intermingled with subzero flurries. Tubal abdomens and long, delicate wings flitted through ambient puddles of the warm-toned, downward beams and back into icy moonlight. The feral flock seemed to have a keen sense of direction, migrating in a menacing cloud of chaos through the streets of Kent upon the frigid wind.

A sudden gust of December air howled through the cracks and crevices of the modest, single-story house, rattling the rafters and shingles with near-hurricane force. Unsecured shutters battered the home's aluminum siding, drumming the dwelling like harrowing wartime gunfire.

From the window, Duncan saw his father's black boots mash up the slick slush on the rotting wood porch. Jack's sneakers, soaked and grass-stained, trailed close behind. The tennis shoes turned. Jack's scream was guttural, oozing with terror.

"What the…? No… No… No! Get 'em off me! Get 'em off!"

With his view partially veiled by a rattling shutter, Duncan caught a glimpse of Randall as he beat Jack with the mud-crusted doormat, slapping their neighbor frantically with the flat, rubber rectangle.

"Jesus, it hurts! They're biting, Bryant! They're gnawing at me!" McKellan shrieked, this time at the insects, his feet spinning in a clumsy circle. "You've taken everything from me! LEAVE US ALONE!"

Randall smashed the door open with a force that sent it ricocheting off the wall behind, back at him.

"They're everywhere!"

Jack erupted over the threshold into the cluttered home, where the stagnant waft of herbal remedies and fresh death now seemed peaceful.

Safe.

McKellan whacked a still-gnashing bug from his jaw and crushed it reflexively into a grimy, braided rug. A wet string of slime traced the path from the fibers to his raised sneaker as he checked beneath the sole to confirm its annihilation.

Randall latched the door securely and yanked Jack to him by the shoulder with violent force. He eyed Randall's open lesions, paying close attention to the bloody openings bored into his exposed skin.

"They get in you?"

"I don't know! I don't know! Jesus, I don't know!"

Randall studied him. "You're lucky. Looks like just flesh wounds."

He released McKellan and ping-ponged across the room, bounding with nervous energy, before landing at the sink. He picked at a days-old hunk of air-dried tortellini on the pile of encrusted dishes.

"Jesus, Duncan. Doesn't your mother ever clean?"

A pause. He flashed his son an apologetic glance for the lack of reverence and incorrect tense of the word.

Jack lumbered to Duncan's post at the bay window and stared at the neighborhood. A wind-like squall of high-pitched insect chitters gnashed through the night air as bugs swarmed his mother's cooling corpse. They dove, wasp-like, mashing their elongated bodies into her head wound, mouth, and any other orifice within reach.

Tanya's body juddered and cracked on the snow-dusted lawn as if disassembled, bone-by-bone, from the inside, like a time-lapse of maggots hollowing out roadkill.

Duncan couldn't avert his eyes as the creatures continued to rattle and render Tanya's corpse as flat as a bearskin rug.

Randall solemnly flipped the overturned dining room table back on its three remaining splintered legs. He tipped a toppled chair upright, sat down, and hugged the backrest.

Jack threw his parka across the couch, its cheap floral pattern now smeared and soaked with rust-colored bloodstains. He bee-lined for the third cupboard in the kitchen, shoving aside a bag of sugar and retrieving a mostly full bottle of tequila. He opened the next grime-coated cabinet and pulled out two shot glasses, wiped them thoroughly with the waistband of his Yale sweatshirt, and smacked each loudly on the countertop.

Randall cringed as Jack prepared drinks in Tanya's kitchen. He was positive McKellan had been one of many men in a long string of 'are-you-going-to-be-my-next-' audition-style trysts Tanya had in the ever-widening radius of the house they once bought to raise a family in. The familiarity McKellan showed around her house only confirmed it.

Jack plopped down a souvenir shot glass with a black bear flashing a peace sign with its furry fingers and joined Randall at the wobbly dining table.

"You know I don't drink anymore. Why would you…?" Randall's soft, disappointed voice trailed off.

"I dunno, Rand, if ever there was a time to fall off the wagon…"

Jack glanced over his shoulder at the insects as they gathered on the bay window. The thick tangle of lanky legs and delicate crimson wings choked out whole patches of the moon and streetlights. He downed the gold liquid, winced, and chased it with a second, searing shot.

Randall toyed with the glass, recalling when he bought it for Tanya on their honeymoon in Denver.

Jack growled and leaned back, chair groaning beneath his imposing frame. "Those things really did a number on this place."

"It wasn't..." Duncan started.

Randall's fierce eyes shot a glance that halted the boy mid-sentence. Duncan turned around and stared at his mother's writhing corpse, wiggling its extremities through a pile of downy pink snow.

"Where the hell did they even come from?" Jack wasn't sure who he was asking.

"They came in on the wind today. Saw 'em during the drive up here. Massive hoard of 'em, blowin' in like a storm. It was like watchin' a red twister rip through the Steins' property down the hill."

Jack pitched his knit beanie on the table and scratched his thick, black hair, graying gracefully near the temples. "What do you think they are?"

Randall opened his thin lips to speak and then smiled as he shut them, opting for silence instead.

Jack arched a thick brow. "What?"

No answer.

He chugged another shot, face contorting.

Randall picked at the flaking bear design on the front of his glass, brimming with yellow booze, which convulsed beneath his touch. "Nah, it's nothing. They just remind me of something. That's all."

Jack poured another shot. "I'm all ears, Bryant."

"Keep your wits about you," Randall warned, motioning to the liquor with mesmerized eyes. He switched subjects, sounding mournful. "So, Candace?"

Jack slid the bottle away. "Jesus, Candace." A new wave of tears seared his reddened eyes. "Yeah, those things... They got her. Swarmed her. Got in her mouth. Choked her. Burrowed 'til they were comin' outta her eyes, for shit's sake!"

He wept so hard that spit dribbled from his mouth, lips frozen in a silent scream.

"Leena, she was just a kid. Not even a teenager yet. Now she's never gonna be! This is insane! This morning, I was eating bland-ass with my wife and daughter, and now..."

After a pause, he grew furious and launched the bottle of tequila against the cabinet. The vessel exploded like a crude bomb packed with wet glass shrapnel.

"What are these things, for Chrissakes?!" Jack howled.

Randall rubbed his strawberry-blond buzz cut and searched for something comforting to say. Found nothing. He gazed at the crowded throng of bugs congregated on the humidity-streaked windows.

"You know, about ten years ago, I was doin' drills down at Camp Shelby down in Mississippi. I used to do all-terrain, off-campus runs down around this nearby area called Leaf River. Sand, gravel, water, grass, you name it. Thought it would make me a better soldier if I was more adaptable to constantly changing terrain. One evening, I'm in the creek, washing off after the run. Nearly sunset. Outta nowhere…" Randall paused and smiled, blue eyes vast and staring. "It's gonna sound far-fetched."

Jack chuckled through spit and tears, tortured over his heavy loss. "After what we saw on the lawn, I doubt it."

Randall waved his boy over and pulled up another overturned chair next to himself. He wiped a smudge of blood off Duncan's face as the child sat.

"So, I'm standing in this muddy river. I'm up to my waist in murky water, lookin' up at the sky. In the distance, I see this… this…shadowy swarm of something advancing on me. It was enormous. Like some gigantic surge of bats or something approaching. Cloud's gettin' thicker. So thick that, as it nears, it starts blocking out the sun. I mean it! This gloomy shade pours over the river, and there are hundreds of thousands… Hell, probably millions of 'em, comin' right at me, covering me in darkness. I have no clue what they are. One hits me right in the cheekbone, and I realize it's a giant fucking bug."

Something thwacked against the window behind him. Duncan winced, afraid to look.

Randall held his fingers open, shy of two inches. "Sucker was this big, easily. I look up. Thousands are swarming me now. They're petrifying. I don't know if they bite. I start smacking myself. They surge on in this tight pack. Tons more latch on. Suddenly, I'm covered in these things. I'm screaming, and they're flying into my mouth. I'm spitting and flailing. I dive into the water and come back up with more latched on my chest. They're everywhere. I can't even breathe without sucking one in my mouth. They're on the bank. In the trees. On my civvies. I keep waiting for them to sting or bite. I'm too panicked to notice if they're doing any damage. This cloud of bugs just looks like some biblical plague."

The glass behind them thumped again.

"I run for my life. I'm crushing 'em, smackin' 'em. I grabbed one and held it in my left hand. Wouldn't let go because, if I did, no one would believe me if I's lucky enough to live to talk about it."

"Holy…" McKellan had the urge to hunt for more booze. "So, what happened?"

"They eventually flocked downriver. Passed me. I started to see the sunset through the bugs as they left. I was shocked. I was unharmed. Unscathed, save for the marks I made smackin' myself. They kept on until the herd of 'em thinned. Their little carcasses were littered all over the river. Half of 'em were now dead and floating, scattered around, stuck in trees like maple seed pods after a storm. All the while, I never let that one in my hand go. Raced back to the barracks. Told my Staff Sergeant. Showed him my souvenir. He laughs his ass off. Tells me they're mayflies. Completely harmless. Don't even have mouths."

Jack chuckled with a spacey glaze to his eyes. "Not like those things out there."

Duncan eyed the bug-peppered window and turned to give his father his full attention.

"He said every May or so, for a single day, they lay larvae in rivers and stuff. Those become water nymphs and eventually transform into this hideous, winged, air-bound insect. They only live for, like, a day. They copulate in massive hordes and race to dump the eggs back in the water before they exhaust themselves and die or get eaten."

Jack's captivated eyes were massive, bloodshot orbs welling up in the corners. "Wild."

Randall pointed over his shoulder with a heavily scarred thumb, marred by combat. "That's what those things remind me of."

"Only these insidious shits are bigger, and they have mouths and teeth." Jack wiped a stray tear from his face.

"Yeah, and burrow and bite," Randall added, his eyes two jumbo, unblinking spheres transfixed with a distant gaze. "Think they mighta been layin' eggs in Tanya when we took her out."

The tap-tap-tapping on the windows grew louder.

Duncan looked war-torn and fried. Lost.

Jack picked at a groove in the table with his fingernail. "Maybe these'll only live for a day, too."

"Let's hope." Randall smoothed his son's bowl-cut brunette locks.

"Even then, though, the damage is done."

"I reckon they're capable of much more than what they've caused already. I mean, hell, we're still here."

Randall slid his shot down the leaning table to Jack, approached the window, widened his stance, and habitually placed his arms behind his back. He stared beyond the scuttling mass at the blustery wind twirling snowflakes around the sodium vapor streetlights perched high overhead.

The whacks against the glass grew hostile. Each noise, a vibrant red insect, four inches long, pounded the fragile single-pane and hung solidly in place. With every smack, the outside lights shining on Randall's face dimmed further.

Thwack! Thwack! Thwack-thwack! Thwack!

They were coming fast, like shells from an automatic rifle now. Even prior to the all-too-familiar sound, Randall knew he was once again at war.

"I'm confused by one thing, though. How the hell did they make that huge gash in her head?" Jack's face soured. He glanced at Duncan, then at Randall, then around at the bedraggled home. "With Candace and Leena, they got in through their mouths, their ears. They took bites and bored little holes and tried to squirm in, like with me out there, but they didn't gouge through bone."

Jack recalled the overturned furniture and the more-than-typical mess in Tanya's home upon his arrival.

His jaw dropped in revelation. "Did you…?"

Randall was matter-of-fact. "I never said those things killed Tanya."

Fury bubbled up in Jack. Eyes pierced like white-hot laser beams. He tilted forward in his chair and assumed an animal posture, ready to attack. "What did you do, Rand?!"

The fit former soldier pressed his back against the cool window, the glass now rattling like a rock concert drum kit and raised his palms. "She was like that when I got here."

Randall's eyes slowly widened, and his expression grew even more grave until McKellan finally pivoted in his creaking chair.

Jack turned just in time to see the rusted hatchet blade before it burst through the tender membrane of his eye, shattering the bony, fragile socket beneath. Hot, garnet-colored fluid spurted across Duncan's face. He swung hard again, this time burying it in Jack's mouth to silence the screams.

One last strike to Jack's throat split him wide. His body shuddered. His hands clutched at the gaping laceration for a prolonged moment. Soon, his arms grew limp and dropped.

The room was enveloped by an eerie silence.

Duncan peered up at his father and relinquished the hatchet, dumping it into the growing, cherry-red pool beneath him.

"I'm sorry, sir." Tears streamed down his youthful cheeks. "I did it again."

Randall watched as his son hid remorsefully among the coats and firewood like a mouse seeking shelter. His unblinking eyes displayed disappointment and fear. His expression mirrored that of sheltered civilians during the regalement of his own most heinous service stories.

Though she was unbearable before, Tanya had become unhinged since the divorce. Her slow crescendo of erratic behavior had terrified them both. He knew how she behaved with him, an adult, and could only fathom what horrors the boy had endured in private. After questioning him earlier, with the child still smeared in Tanya's blood, it was clear he'd unquestionably paid the price for his father's sins.

As a killer himself, having taken numerous lives overseas — some under orders and some cannon fodder — Randall decided he had little room to judge the boy.

In a way, he and Duncan were now entrenched in the same war. A new war. One fought against a ravenous hoard of skittering, ruddy parasites ripping through a once-quiet municipality upon the biting winter wind. A town he had wrongly deemed safe enough to start a family in a decade ago.

A town now full of bloodshed, painted in vermilion.

Like the other witnessed atrocities performed outside the mission boundaries during active service, he was willing to take his young fellow soldier's deadly secrets to the grave. Which, at the rate the light was disappearing from the bay window, might not be far away.

SATED

My humble little burger joint is packed and bustling with vibrant energy tonight. I've given my life to Buzz's Burgers, and now several others have done the same. Though in those instances, unknowingly.

I used to ask fellow restaurateurs here in New England for recommendations on quality leads for local ground beef. In retrospect, even their best suggestions paled in comparison to the sinfully delicious products I currently serve, though procurement is a more tedious process these days. I size up every patron that walks in the door, my welcoming eyes locked on their thighs to imagine the marbling of fat beneath their clothing.

It's proven to be a choice cut, time and again.

I stare as they jam their mouths with crispy bacon, ripe avocado slices, and fried onion strings, washing them down with carbonated colas slurped through green paper straws. The customers have grown tolerant of them, and we hate to create waste here. On that same subject, I often find myself lost in thought, questioning if I'm wasting any cuts of grind-able meat on the pigs.

It's astonishing that ol' Mitchell hasn't noticed his animals fattening despite feeding them the bare minimum. I wonder if he's any inkling that, for a month, his sows have helped cover up several heinous sins.

My deviant extra-curricular activity is exhausting atop my regular workload. Surprisingly, one thing I don't have to worry about is the repentant moral wrestling of these activities. Ironically enough, mom raised me — God rest her soul — to be a wholesome, upstanding Catholic boy.

But here I am.

No longer wholesome.

Laughably upstanding…

Lost in a daydream about what the man's biceps at table four would look like flayed on the table behind me.

I peer out the kitchen doors as Allie serves the four their meals. A blackened blue and a roadhouse cheeseburger, two house specialties here at my Connecticut dive, tucked in a run-down strip mall between the Happy Days Nail Salon and Lance's Gym on a main thoroughfare, choosing the spot because I thought the wafting smell of my juicy, grilled burgers would tempt the starving, string-bean women and muscle-bound lunkheads to cheat on their diets.

This was not the case.

Since I started a year and a half ago, business steadily dwindled. My investment fell apart day by day as I watched gym rats race on their wheels through the glass front of their building across the corner of the parking lot from my empty restaurant.

Over the last few months, business slowed to a crawl. I went underwater on the bills and paying purveyors. I spent money constantly at the printers on stacks of flyers for the windshields in the parking lot, offering discounts that would sweeten the deal if these health-conscious nuts would give my burgers a chance.

I hemorrhaged money.

The diner went on life-support. I borrowed money from my folks in Florida to keep the doors open. I laid off Jimmy, the other line cook I'd hired, plus my hostess, Theresa, and two of the remaining three waiters, Andy and Mel.

The look on their crushed faces killed me.

I felt like some dead-beat father who failed his children. Someone who battered them before putting them on the sidewalk to fend for themselves.

However, the real turn of events started three weeks ago…

By accident.

…Sort of.

Accident is the wrong word. Kismet might be more appropriate. I'm a believer in fate.

Or maybe it was divine intervention. I believe in that, too.

God works in mysterious ways.

Herbert Looper never should've come in with his tiny, stupid notebook and smug half-grin, eager to put this wounded burger joint out of its misery with a .9 mm to the forehead.

I abhor critics. They often have little idea how difficult it is to make the inventive food they shit on... and to cook it to the same standards consistently. He came to smear my name. To do damage that would cause internal bleeding that I'd be unable to stop.

Oh, the irony.

Before closing one day — it was the 4th, which I only remember because some bills were due and my vegetable purveyor called and vowed to cut me off until I paid in full — Looper came in, ordered a couple of our top sellers (the truffle portobello and Tillamook-Swiss burger, and the habanero pepper-jack turkey burger, if I recall) and jotted down his snarky thoughts and half-hearted observations. I watched him through the holes in the swing doors, my eyes searing into him like the sizzling grill behind me into raw, ground beef.

I knew who he was after seeing his photos in some local Milford 40-under-40 spreads. Hard to forget those thick-rimmed wayfarers, Hawaiian shirts, and hipster-coiffed, greasy black hair. Half my age and with a cocky smile that seemed permanently fused on his face beneath his well-groomed beard.

That fateful Tuesday night, he remained in the dining room after he paid the tab for the two medium-well masterpieces he barely touched. I'd come out, stood at his table, and asked how the meal was. He didn't respond verbally. Just bounced his bold, black eyebrows and nodded a little. I made some sort of joke about him being hungry enough to eat for two, and I remember he forced a half-smile and a phony-sounding scoff, and then he held up his cup, insinuating he wanted a refill. I obliged, clinging tightly to my smile and returning with the full drink before slinking back into my kitchen to steal glances behind the barrier.

Candace cashed him out, hung up her apron, waved goodbye, and went home to her kid, Nigel. He's two. Good kid. Whenever he's here, I make his favorite (the Bayou Heat Burger, blackened, with boudin balls on the side. That kid loves those boudin balls.)

After she left, I cleaned off the grill and started scrubbing down all the surfaces of the kitchen. I don't go home until it's clean enough to eat a burger off the floor. A light rap on one of the swinging doors took me by surprise. Through the oval window, Looper's dark, beady eyes and thick eyebrows glared in at me. He murmured something. He was asking to come in. I obliged, hoping to secure a positive impression and show off my small but immaculate kitchen, the cleanliness of which is something I have always taken immense pride in.

I remember him scoping the place out, touching surfaces, and looking inside appliances while he spoke to me with horrifying candor about how "subpar" my food was and babbled on about the inferior quality of my ground beef, suggesting locally sourced grass-fed beef instead. I informed him that it was (and that we pay more for it), and he stared at me incredulously. He droned on about the greasiness, and I zoned out, his words no longer audible to me. His condescending smile told me he relished the unearned feeling of superiority.

I don't remember my hand ever picking up the cleaver.

I just remember smashing into the back of his neck with it as he started out the doors, burying it deep in muscle and hardened vertebrae. He dropped to the floor, his feet unresponsive as he clamored for the door, smearing my freshly mopped tile with a pool of his thick, pathetic blood.

A sickening mix of fury and satisfaction bubbled up in my rib cage as the sharpened implement tore into his meat and spinal column a few more times.

I recall heaving and struggling to catch my breath with total clarity. I watched the weak, dying twitches of his body in the growing puddle of garnet blood with fascination as Death's outstretched black hand ushered him from this world. His head was nearly severed from his spine. Multiple hack marks exposed marred vertebrates and raw, clean-cut musculature.

I'd never experienced classic Catholic guilt overtaking me. This shocked me.

Instead, I only felt a heart-pounding ferocity.

I have sunk every penny, every spare moment of time, every hope and aspiration, into Buzz's Burgers, and there was no way I could allow him to blow a hole in my boat and sink this place with foul judgments based on one dining experience.

When he'd dogged the quality of my "subpar meat," it made me recant my days as a butcher in my twenties at a big chain grocery store in Hartford that changed ownership and names several times. My buddy, Kevin, and I used to slice ham and joke about grinding up whiny customers. We laughed about serving them by the pound with a steep price tag labeled "long pig" right there in the window. We wondered if anyone would buy it and laughed about scenarios in which rampant sales of it would revitalize the floundering chain.

The night Looper laid face down in his own life fluids, choking on raspy drags of dying breath, I went a step further. I had to get rid of the body to avoid losing everything, including my freedom. Yet another part of me craved the opportunity to experiment with a new ingredient, which, as a restaurateur, is something I have always done without apology. People always want something fresh and new that adheres to the comfort a classic format provides.

It was so satisfying to carve off slivers of his flesh and to churn hunks of his face, ass, and calves through my two-year-old shiny little meat grinder, pulverizing and seasoning him. He was placed onto racks, reduced to metal trays full of perfectly seasoned paper-wrapped patties in my walk-in fridge.

In the wee hours of the morning, I burned his clothes in my fire pit at home and emptied the garbage sacks of bones and leftover useless parts (ears and fingers, etc.) over my neighbor's fence and stared, unblinking, as Mitchell's swine annihilated his remains. Any remaining trace of him had been decimated by those sows, hungrily crunching their way through the youthful critic's hardened bone and gristle with sickening, sloppy sounds.

I couldn't stop myself that afternoon when we opened for lunch. Despite being weary from only three hours of sleep and aching from all the extra physical exertion, I grew giddy at the thought of adding the new special to the menu.

Much to my surprise, the long pig burger I dubbed The Critic was a massive success with the few regulars that remained. They raved, returning the next day with friends. Several gym rats also caved. One runner, still slick with sweat, said he caught a whiff of our sizzling "beef" in the parking lot and couldn't help himself.

Within four days, I was fresh out of Long Pig. I feared business would again dwindle. But by a stroke of luck, a Milford Health Inspector soon paid me a visit.

I think something might be wrong with me.

I should feel remorse or guilt, but instead of biting my nails and having nightmares about these despicable acts, I'm actually excited about the future of this humble little burger joint.

As I look out these oval windows at the mastication taking place beyond the door, people stuffing their grinning maws with an exotic kind of ground meat, I remember this is what it's all about.

I started this business to give customers sustenance they enjoy, and I've done just that.

I'm going to keep the long pig on the menu. The swine at the Mitchell's will continue to eat well, their rotund bellies swelling with the weight of my sins for as long as I'm allowed to carry on. Though there's no real way to "ethically source" this protein, I'll constantly make adjustments to minimize how little goes to waste. Maybe I'll add a delectable bone broth soup to the menu served in a crock with oyster crackers and torch-fired cheese around the rim. Or use oils from the brains to add flavor to the sausage links I plan to add when I change the hours to include the breakfast crowd, too.

Beyond these windowed, metal doors that separate me from the thrilled customers lining up at the hostess station, our tables are packed full of sated gluttonous patrons, all patting their satisfied bellies and leaving Candace, Andy, Mel, and our newest hire (to accommodate the increase in lunch and dinner traffic,) Allie, generous tips.

Seems they're really enjoying the inspector.

If my mother — God rest her soul — could see me now, remorselessly serving people to their fellow man, she'd be rolling over in her grave.

Burying our dead is such a strange, uneconomical concept to me now. Graves... what a waste of good meat.

IN THE BLOOD

OF THE MARTYR

Odessa leaned against the thin, coal-black rail, forcing a perfectly even divide up the granite steps, and admired the slender cross towering overhead. It floated peacefully on the snow-dusted spire like the cherry-red plastic shell itself had just been called up to Heaven for the rapture.

Soft flakes danced around her, shaken down from the stormy, charcoal sky like a barrel of blowing glitter. There were no clouds, only a darkened backdrop to contrast the fine crystals composing a suffocating haze. She watched as a small murder of crows congregated on the snowy lawn between the church and forest, wings closely tucked. They stoically stamped clawed feet through the fluff and scoured the area with soured onyx faces like drill soldiers scrutinizing boot camp barracks.

The surrounding woods and their tangle of gnarled, leafless oak branches slicing through the fog offered the humble church a cloak of immense seclusion. Beyond the modest structure, fresh flurries muffled the often sharp and foreboding sounds of the wilderness. There were no howling canines or hoot owls running amok today. No, today it was quiet.

So quiet.

Odessa checked her watch and focused her gaze back on the building. There it stood before her - just as it always had - in the crisp, January air, looming erect above her slender frame in all its glory:

The doors to salvation.

The two weighty double doors arched together like two hands pressed in heartfelt prayer. Odessa could draw their ornate angelic embellishments from memory if she had to. The immense detail in them offset the building's otherwise drab exterior. She stared at the carved wooden sun beaming its sharp, precise rays onto smiling winged cherubs frolicking beneath.

Sometimes, she wondered if she loved those doors as much as their creator must've.

Ronald rounded the corner from the gravel parking lot on the side, brushing past the trunk of a crooked oak and stopping, entranced by a huge freshly dug trough of dirt. Hunks of frozen umber soil trailed across the drift beside it, defiling the true white blanket of snowfall and tainting its purity. He glanced down at the long pit and sucked in a deep breath before smiling weakly across the snow-strewn lawn at Odessa. His ebony dress shoes crunched up the shoveled path, grinding against the rock salt.

He matched her height and cocked his head similarly to see the church through her eyes. The proximity made her writhe reflexively toward the handrail. Ronald backed away, letting out a terribly nervous chuckle.

"I'm sorry," he offered, raising his hands in surrender, his voice soft and thickly coated in sincerity.

Odessa pinched her lips together and shook her head to imply, 'No, it's fine.' The snow was coming down harder now, in chunkier clusters, as if the weather was somehow as affected by Ronald's presence as she was.

"It's so good to see you," the man cooed.

Odessa tried to force a half-smile, but it came out more like the first warning snarl of an apprehensive designer dog. She wished she could say the same of him, but she simply couldn't. And she wasn't about to spout lies and false niceties, not on the steps of a place so holy.

Not today, of all days.

She peered at Ronald's pricey coal-black overcoat dappled with frozen precipitation like he was being seasoned by a God-sized shaker. Like it could, in some way, possibly make him more palatable.

"You're dressed nice." Odessa's voice sounded tiny through the noise-dampened snowfall. It was the best, truest thing her winter-chapped lips could utter.

"Thank you." Ronald took a deep, anxious sigh. "It's a big day."

And he was right.

His all-too-familiar voice whirled through her brain like eggs being scrambled with a whisk.

A big day, indeed.

"You look lovely," Ronald added. His cheeks rose, and his smile was soft. He glanced quickly down at her attire. "Really suits you, that dress." His expression faded, replaced rapidly by melancholy. He cleared his throat and coughed into his gloved fist. "Seeing you in white right now… it's a real shame I'll never get to watch you walk down the aisle."

"You did this to yourself."

She couldn't believe she said it. Not aloud, anyway. Her tone was chilling.

"You're right." He affectionately wiped some clinging flakes from her bob of dirty-dishwater colored hair.

She tensed.

"I thought I made myself clear." Her voice was a meek growl with a definite tinge of seeping hatred. Odessa flexed her arms at her sides and frowned, noticing more parishioners plowing their own deep, snowy paths around the trough.

"It was melting," Ronald mumbled gently, "I'm sorry. I couldn't help myself."

I'm sorry. I couldn't help myself.

The words made Odessa want to throw up right on the stone steps in front of the place she deemed most sacred. Or scream. Or cry. Or rip up the thin rail she was pressed against and beat him with it. She pictured herself towering over his rotund body afterward, his troubled face round and pale, as much from the treacherous cold as the brutal abuse, with thick violet rings forming around his battered, blackening eyes as he begged her over and over to stop. She'd look down, laugh, and mutter the same:

I'm sorry. I couldn't help myself.

She tried to soothe herself. After all, soon she'd never have to hear him emit those useless syllables — or any syllables —ever again.

Closure.

Ahhh, that would be divine.

From around the corner, Nina shuffled up. Though active in worship, she was a well-known curmudgeon. In New England, her southern accent advertised how far from home she'd found herself. "Is that... Ron?"

Ronald grinned and nodded.

"It's been years!" Nina's simple, no-nonsense slip-on shoes made their agonizingly slow path up the concrete until the two estranged acquaintances were finally tip-toed in a sincere embrace. Puffy blobs of white fluff landed in her sparse hair of matching colorlessness. Even this early in the morning, mingling with the aroma of the vanilla musk perfume she must've bathed in, Ronald could still smell faint traces of beer on the old woman's breath as she strained up to kiss him on the cheek. She wiped the trace smudges of mauve lipstick from his face and released him from her bony clutches.

"It's so good to see you. We are so glad to have you back! What kept you away from us for so long?" Nina swatted him in the arm with her frail, age-spotted hand.

Ronald dodged the question, responding instead by saying, "Let's get you both inside where it's warm, shall we?" He offered up his elbow to the women politely.

Nina took it. Odessa didn't. She started toward the doors, subtly refusing the gentlemanly gesture.

She wanted to get this over with, and yet, another part of her wanted it to last forever.

The twisted handle of the left door was so icy in her slight, bare hand the brass surface was shocking. She forced the groaning door open and laid her almost colorless hazel eyes on the seats inside. Despite the frostiness of the temperature outside, her body was instantly injected with a warm sense of ease.

Salvation.

A comforting wash of divinity and redemption would douse her soon, like a hot rain of truth and love and forgiveness, dripping down across her flesh, coating her newly reborn body.

She couldn't wait. Her nerves tingled.

She would be birthed anew. Cleansed of all past transgressions, be they her fault or not. Rejuvenated. As sinless, once again, in the eyes of the Lord as she had been the day she was born.

She'd be one massive step closer to spending eternity in Heaven above, cradled in the arms of God.

***

The songs in celebration of the Pentecost raged on, and Odessa squirmed in her seat as all the minutes of the sermon and Sunday traditions ticked past. She was too excited about what would punctuate the end of it all to focus on the messages in the text.

Somewhere amid the second song, she stripped her long coat off and draped it over the back of her conjoined chair to allow for a freer range of arm movements. She was cognizant of Ronald's gaze lingering on her body, swearing she could feel it searing to the naked flesh beneath her clothes. Moments later, she saw his thick pinky stretching to touch the supple skin of her hand, which was clasped around the side of her closely connected chair. When she saw it, she raised her hands and rattled her wrists like her palms were maracas. This way, she could sense the Lord's light shining through her body and, with Ronald, maintain some plausible deniability.

Odessa offered up her vocal cords, as she often did, to the Holy Spirit and began to vocalize. She turned off her mind and became a vessel from which the deity spoke:

La ah tee sha na na net ee pah sha na cue.

Can a de dee pah nee ha ma drah!

The glossolalial utterances spewed out of her mouth at the Holy Ghost in a frenzy of mishmashed syllables so Satan would not be able to understand or intercept her scrambled transmission.

Pen a tet a ka sha ma na na na.

Pah det a tee tah men ah pet a cue can a tet droo gah…

Her eyes rolled back, and she became dissociated from the church, its short rows of interlocked chairs, and the other thirty or so parishioners in praise. She uttered the jumbled, secretive syllables to the Lord. The Pentecostals had always taught her the clever improvisation of speaking in tongues was key to confusing eavesdropping demons.

Ronald leaned over to whisper something to her, but his voice didn't register. Instead of repeating himself, he eased back, smiled kindly, and pressed his hands into the air. Odessa muttered on, murmuring words in gibberish toward the ceiling.

Det pa nee tah ven too be rosque a ma na thah dev.

Eel es gon a geh ch yah ah het a due!

Everyone in the church had their hands up in jubilant spiritual worship. In the front row, Gladys, a devout, joyful woman whom Odessa had been acquainted with for decades, began to shake and shudder. Her beaded bracelets jingled with the vibrations.

Several God-fearing men and women engulfed in praise cried out, their tones shrill and chilling. But they weren't terrified. They were cheerfully overjoyed. They, too, were overwhelmed by the Holy Spirit.

A threatening darkness tumbled into the country sky and oozed in through the rectangular stained-glass windows. The shaking faces of people deeply reverent near the carpeted side aisles flickered with every color of the rainbow.

The pastor, Arthur Wallace, was front and center with his arms the highest, molding the group deeper into their collective hysteria. He was middle-aged now, though he was only a teenager when Odessa started attending Fellowship Pentecost as a young girl.

The pious man proved to be a pillar of comfort for her through her darkest times. The years when God tested her faith to prove the strength of her fidelity, as he had Job's. Though it was the hardest time of her life, she passed the test. She never lost her loyalty to God, even when the demon came to her in the form of a human. Even when that human stripped her of her purity like an ungodly, towering beast... night after night.

Wallace had been there for her, teaching her the Lord's word throughout those tribulations. He taught Sunday school back then as his father, Neil Wallace, had been the church's pastor. Now, the salvation of the fellowship lay rightfully in Arthur's hands.

Hands blessed by God.

Today, Pastor Wallace wore a dress shirt, crisp alabaster slacks, and a matching white blazer. It was a ceremonious day, and he knew the Lord would prefer he dressed as such. He took off the jacket and charged up the center aisle between the pews, speaking his own disguised words to God in tongues. He raged utterances in a menacing tone, growling and roiling about Satan's hold on the God-fearing people of their undeniably treacherous, yet decidedly salvageable, town.

Piercing cries and gasps rolled out over the crescendo of voices coming from the roaring choir, relentlessly scream-singing their bouncy hymns of God's glory over the Pastor's nonsensical vocalizations.

The pastor whipped his white jacket at some parishioners, smacking violently like a lion tamer's whip. It was as though he might slap the sin right out of them. From the abrupt absence of the moral weight of their infractions, they collapsed to the floor in a unified wave of bodies.

Lawrence, a boyishly attractive twenty-something who'd attended the church since he was practically born, savagely shook in the center aisle behind Wallace as if electrocuted. His father, John, the sleepy town's Sheriff, beamed with pride at the sight. He shoved his hands into the air to praise the glory of God for his son's convulsions.

Pastor Wallace raced up to Lawrence and stood face-to-face, hollering in tongues.

Pet cer a tum na kah she fa na fa fa be cet a que le nep ah nit!

Dee fa nah a ten ah pa dru go ne he pah cer ah the nooh can a tet!

He rammed his palm hard against Lawrence's forehead, knocking the young man backward into a gaggle of adults in their Sunday best, trampling each other to catch him. They sprawled Lawrence across the floor, and he seized recklessly. The pastor bolted on with a surge of excited energy, then slowed again, this time at Odessa's row.

Wallace held out a firm, righteous hand, and, with her heart racing, she took it.

This was it.

This was her moment. At last, she would become pure. She would be whole.

In the Lord's eyes... and in her own.

Pastor Wallace extended his other hand to Ronald, extracting him from the aisle after her. A manic rush of excitement aerated through Odessa's blood, percolating into her brain, swishing around like the woozy wash of total intoxication.

Pastor Wallace led them both toward the stage. They stepped over Lawrence's heaving body on the floor, still rattling like the tail of a defensive, agitated serpent. The trio halted, and Wallace released their palms. They waited patiently near the stairs.

Wallace sauntered up to the middle of the stage and, with dramatic, feathered downward hand motions, signaled his desire for the choir's decrescendo. Their pure set of voices lulled to a quiet, spiritual hum of gospel. Gooseflesh spread across Odessa's skin, paired with a shiver that shook her to the core.

Thunder cracked, sending long, resounding ripples of noise trailing through the humid morning air. Odessa could see through the transparent, colorless spots in the stained glass that the snow had ceased, replacing itself with a troubled sky fraught with blackened nimbostratus clouds. But inside, a trance of unfettered power and grace surged through the frenzied Pentecostals. Pastor Wallace took the mic.

"Ladies and gentlemen, today is a special day; yes, it is. Rise to your feet. Yes. Rise with the strength of the Lord, like his true, almighty spirit is traveling through your body and resting you safely on them, Amen." The pastor spoke in long, uncontrolled, run-on sentences whenever his words to the Holy Spirit spewed forth.

Answering a question in unison that hadn't been asked, the crowd muttered their varied amens in unison.

The sheriff tugged Lawrence to his feet gently. Gladys raised her hands high and returned to her treasured spot in the front of the assembly. The dog pile of people recomposed themselves, smiling brightly, patting one another on the backs, and shaking hands in fellowship. The choir of older women hummed on with wholesome, virtuous voices, providing Wallace with the perfect soundtrack for his ceremony.

"Today is a new day, about forgiveness, yes it is, it's about forgiveness, it's about rebirth, yes it is, it's about strength and righting the wrongs the Devil wants us to do, but we will rise above, won't we?"

Dozens of 'Amens' and 'Praise Jesuses' arose through the congregation. The choir grew louder. "We must fight with our eternal souls to keep Satan out of us and in Hell where he belongs, and we are only human, but God watches over us, God protects us, he does, yes, and God wants you to be pure, yes he does. He wants us all to be pure. When we move on to the most glorious place there is, he does not want us to track our filth into his home."

"No, he doesn't! No, sir!" Nina shouted at the top of her lungs, doubling over her short, frail frame, with her wrinkled eyes clamped shut and her ancient, crepe-paper hands uplifted.

"No, he doesn't," Odessa said, locking her steely, tear-welled gaze on Ronald.

"God... he's given us a unique opportunity to cleanse ourselves, our souls. He's blessed us with the ability to wipe our troubled slate clean whenever we want if we just..." He left them hanging. "If you just believe, you see, if we believe that he will grant us true forgiveness, then we can start anew, fresh as a newborn baby without a single sin. He wants us… to… give our troubles to him. He has given us the opportunity to revile our past transgressions, you see, and to recommit ourselves to him through baptism; praise Jesus, yes, he does."

"Praise Jesus!" the sheriff shouted, his hands raised like he was in a stick-up. "Praise Jesus, yes. Amen!"

Pastor Wallace brought Odessa and Ronald on stage. He situated Ronald in front of the central podium, plucked up the microphone, and reverently addressed his congregation.

"Tertullian wrote... in the second century that..." He held his pause a long time for dramatic effect. "He wrote that... the blood of martyrs is the seed of the Church. Now, what does that mean: the seed of the church?" Their eyes were lit. They awaited the answer hungrily. "That, ladies and gentlemen, means a martyr's willing sacrifice of their life can lead to the conversion of others, and well, folks, there's no nobler cause to life than leading to the salvation of the soul of another."

The church fell silent except for Lawrence, who bellowed out, still entranced, "Amennnnn-ah! Praise Jesus!"

"The Bible says this as well, doesn't it?"

"Mmmm-hmmmm!" Gladys hummed aloud through the rhetorical silence.

"In fact, in John, chapter fifteen, verse thirteen, John says: Greater love has no one than this than to lay down one's life for his friends, does he not?" He paused and then reiterated, "…than to lay down one's life for his friends."

A hush blanketed the assembly. The angelic choir powered on.

"So what do these two writings mean? Well, they very clearly mean that a martyr's willing sacrifice can lead... to the salvation of others." His bipolar inflections wavered from stern to tender — and back again.

"Amen!" Nina howled.

Pastor Wallace's tone grew suddenly frenzied and raw. "Blessed be, God! That is a glorious thought, is it not, folks?! The fact that God would allow such simple creations like us, his blessed flock, to salvage a soul from DAMNATION and to have control of the eternal SALVATION of another that is a blessing, is it not? That is a truly almighty gift he has bestowed upon us, his children."

The decibel level of the choir's song increased. Pastor Wallace's expression switched dramatically to stoic. He placed the microphone in the holder in front of the podium where Ronald stood. Wallace gave him an extended, vise-like hug and leaned toward the mic again.

"I believe most of you know Ronald Jeffrey. He's been a member of Word since, well, since I was teaching Sunday school and daddy was the pastor." The crowd emitted a rumble of nostalgic chuckles.

"Many of you haven't seen Ronald here for a while. Ronald felt shame and guilt and, therefore, turned from the Lord and from this assembly. But Ronald came to me a few months back, seeking private council. Seeking guidance from the church. He's done some things he seeks absolution from. And I'm here to tell you no sin is unforgivable in the eyes of the Lord."

Though she believed it to be factual, Odessa's stomach spun like a high-speed rock tumbler grinding down the hardened texture of those last few words.

Wallace continued, the overhead par-cans flashing pure white sparkles across his sincere eyes. "Absolution can only be found in the truth. s six, chapter twenty-two says: But now you have been set free from sin and have become slaves of God. It says the benefit you reap leads to holiness, and the result is... eternal life. For the wages of sin is death, but the gift of God is eternal life in Christ Jesus, our Lord. Now, I think that's a pretty clear message, don't you?"

The assembly offered solemn nods and higher palms.

"Ronald here has got something he wants off his chest before we absolve him in the eyes of the

Lord, isn't that right, Ronald?" Wallace patted the man on the back with his palm and flashed a glance as if to say, it's okay, you're safe here.

Ronald stepped timidly to the podium and coughed. "I apologize. I don't really know how to start this." He took a deep breath and nervously exhaled.

Tell them all what Satan made you do, you monster...

Odessa stared blankly at his hands atop Wallace's closed King James bible. Ronald caressed the leather cover of it with his meaty fingers. He ran them up and down the textured material to soothe himself, but the sight of him tenderly touching it wrenched her gut hard like a wrung sponge.

Tell them.

Tell them all.

"I've... I... I'm not well. You see, for many years... I allowed Satan's influence. I allowed it in my life and also into my stepdaughter's life. I allowed the Devil to... I allowed him into my mind... into my heart, and... in doing so, I took away a young girl's innocence. This young woman trusted me." He put a hand on Odessa's shoulder. She permitted it but stared off, not emoting. His complexion had surpassed beet red from the embarrassment. His gut flipped, and he feared he'd soon have a full audience whilst puking.

He took a deep breath to quell the nausea. "She looked up to me like a father, and in many ways, I was. I waged war against my own sinful thoughts for a while. But when she turned ten, I began to get deviant and shameful... urges... and..." Shame-filled tears rained from Ronald's eyes. "I allowed Satan… to win."

His voice quivered, and his hands shook above the bible. He couldn't believe he was admitting his darkest secrets so publicly to the entire assembly, even though this confession had been the plan for weeks. He was vile, and he could feel lustful thoughts of her still faintly coursing through the darkened folds of his sick mind. This was the first time he'd genuinely felt the gravity of just how despicably wretched his actions were. His brain whirled with thoughts of remorse for the damning things he'd done to Odessa when she was so young, so trusting, all for his own pleasure. He collapsed to his elbows on the podium in pure disgust over the gold-edged bible. His tears pattered on the leather.

"I did things to that poor, sweet little girl. For years, I robbed her of—" Sobbing hard, he howled out, "I... I couldn't help myself!"

There were those words again.

The sickening words that deflected all the appalling guilt and responsibility for his loathsome actions. The ones insinuating he was totally powerless to restrain himself even as a girl of ten... twelve... fifteen begged him to please, dear God, stop! Words whose power paled in comparison to how tirelessly her tiny body fought to buck his massive frame off her.

They were the words of a coward.

You could've helped yourself, you sick—

Wallace put his hand on Ronald's shoulder to illustrate to the congregation that he was a man deserving of forgiveness. Odessa felt numb now. Watching Ronald blubber over what he'd consciously, soberly done so many times... over so many inexcusable years...

Those tears, whether real or crocodile, were useless to Odessa now.

"She said to me before we walked in today, she said I did this to myself. And she's right. I don't have the right to blame her for still being angry for all these years. I tried for over ten years to become a better man. And I did. But I put myself... I put both of us in this position now, and God has given me a chance to right those wrongs."

Ronald coughed again, wincing, and wiped a stray tear. "Pastor Wallace and I have been involved in private counseling the last few months, as many of you have been, I'm sure. He told me about Tertullian's writings, and it only made sense that baptism would be the way to save our souls. Thank you, Pastor Wallace, for this amazing opportunity to give Odessa the gift of her purity back."

Pastor Wallace nodded, pleased, and took the microphone. "God's grace is amazing, it really is. This man is prostrating himself before you good members of the congregation. Members he's known for decades. He asks not just for your forgiveness... but for the Lord's forgiveness. Ronald is about to make the ultimate gesture of goodwill to ensure that God grants that forgiveness." Pastor Wallace blotted the side of his mouth with a white handkerchief. "At this time, I'd love to get the baptismal tub out here. Can we do that?"

Lawrence and another young man around the same age sprung up from the mass of people and stepped to the stage's left wing toward a massive object on casters. They pulled some shimmery purple fabric off, revealing a bathtub full of water on a wooden platform. Wallace moved the podium and mic stand away as they wheeled it front-and-center and locked the wheels.

They stood, hands clasped, behind it, awaiting orders like soldiers.

Pastor Wallace led Ronald in front of the tub and whispered for the man to strip. Odessa struggled to focus. The site of the man peeling off his clothes again made her woozy and nauseous. She glanced away, completely unable to watch.

The two young men broke away and, on the floor beside the casters, rolled out a hefty sheet of painter's plastic. One handed Wallace a briefcase.

Once stripped to his tight, white underwear, the men helped Ronald in the water. He stood, legs together and arms outstretched like a hairy, overweight savior. The men hooked their elbows beneath his armpits and clutched forcefully upward. But Ronald didn't struggle. Wallace opened the case, pulling out a knife with a long, sharpened blade. He offered it up in his flattened palms as a Catholic priest would hold a Holy Communion chalice.

He stepped behind Ronald. The choir's voices thundered through the small church. Ronald could sense the vibrations of their opus in his thudding chest.

"Will it hurt?" Ronald asked, experiencing momentary second thoughts.

Odessa feared the thought of him backing out.

No, don't do this!

"No, Ronald. Eternity in Heaven will feel like bliss. This shell you were born with... it won't matter anymore. You'll be with God." Wallace assured him and whispered something else into his ear. "I envy you so much."

And he did.

Ronald took a deep breath through tears and mouthed to Odessa, "I love you." She did not want to be a hypocrite. She'd been pummeled with nearly two decades of sermons on how God wanted his children to love one another. Still, she couldn't physically bring herself to return the sentiment, not even as a lie to ease him in his final moments.

The men tightened their grips, and Pastor Wallace gouged the knife into the depths of Ronald's throat. He sliced it all the way across, chanting aloud to the Holy Spirit. Sanguine blood spewed from the raw meat within Ronald's gaping, mortal wound. The tub water churned, changing from soft blue to vibrant crimson. His heavy, heaving body gasped and choked. His submerged feet thrashed.

Pastor Wallace whipped out his white handkerchief and put a corner in each of the young men's pinched fingers. They held it away from the open gash to shield the worshipers from the brutal carnage and the carpet from the forceful air-born spurts.

"Lord, I ask that you bless Ronald. Bless this man martyred here before you as he joins you in the kingdom of power and glory."

Blood sputtered from Ronald's wide-open carotid. It coated his hairy chest and filled the severed hole in the center of his throat, suffocating his whistling gasps for air. The two unfazed men struggled to hold his hefty, quaking body. Their once-pristine church attire, along with the outer shell of the tub, became stained in an almost coordinated set of dripping viscous burgundy stripes.

"Lord Jesus, we ask that the blood of your lamb be his ultimate sacrifice... the sacrifice needed to free him and... and... purify him of all that Satan asked him to do, Heavenly Father. We ask you to wash his soul clean, Lord, and we beg that for every drop that spills from him, Holy Spirit, that that blood be the conductor to the salvation of others."

Ronald seized with ferocity and coughed blood across Wallace's cheek. The pastor didn't flinch.

Flecked in crimson, he continued into the microphone over the random praises shouted by the people in attendance. "He gives himself unto you now, oh Lord, freely and without reservation. Lord, we ask that you take Ronald from us now, not as a man, but as an offering in exchange for the salvation of your child here on earth." Wallace placed a blood-flecked arm around Odessa.

She smiled, her heart full of newfound joy and renewed hope.

Wallace held the mic to his lips, muttering the prayer just louder than the voices of the choir. "We ask, oh Holy Spirit, that you accept this ultimate sacrifice, Lord, as the seed of the Church so that we may purify your daughter as well."

Odessa raised her hands, thrilled by the glorious sight of Ronald's body as it fell slack. "Praise Jesus!" Relief crested over her in an oceanic wave and crashed down into ecstasy.

Thunder cracked close to the discreet building, and a few parishioners gasped like they'd just heard the booming voice of God and his undeniable approval of this glorious occasion rattling the foundation. A gleaming shaft of light burst through the window, bathing Ronald momentarily in the arctic glow of the lightning strike. The momentary illumination lit up the pain in his contorted face. It was a sight that made

Odessa absolutely giddy. She watched closely as the last of his life faded from his cider-brown irises.

Eyes she knew all too well from years of intimacy.

The shuddering ceased. Pastor Wallace flashed Odessa a blood-freckled smile.

It was her turn.

Finally.

Wallace nodded to her, and she slowly unzipped her stained white dress. She let it slink to the short carpet beneath her feet. For the first time, her nudity wasn't a crime. Ronald was dead. He was with the Lord now. And no one would ever leer provocatively at her nakedness in that way again.

The men dragged Ronald's flaccid corpse out of the tub and laid him down reverently on the painter's plastic. They crossed his hands over his chest and tactfully rolled and tucked it around him like they were swaddling a newborn.

Pastor Wallace held out a hand to Odessa. She took it for leverage and stepped into the merlot-colored water. She faced the congregation, her breasts heaving with the movements of her shallow, excited breathing.

"Heavenly Father, we thank you for your presence here in this holy place. Lord, we are grateful that we feel so powerful and vital today, God."

Odessa lowered to her knees and allowed the garnet liquid to swallow her body. She sat fully and extended her legs forward as much as the small bath would allow. Pastor Wallace kneeled on the rear of the platform near her.

Wallace placed a hand on her shoulder and closed his eyes. "God, we thank you for your devotional child, oh Lord. Odessa is making a commitment today to dedicate her life entirely to you, God. We praise you, Lord, and praise that you will change her life immensely, Heavenly Father, as she gives herself to you through baptism in the blood of the martyr, Lord. Lord, we ask that you fulfill her prayer when she comes back up out of this baptism of the Holy Ghost; oh, we ask this from you in the name of Jesus Christ."

Wallace handed the microphone off to one of the young men and spoke right to the steeping woman. He lovingly smoothed down her dirty blonde hair with a calm hand and caressed her cheek.

"Odessa, upon the confession of your faith in the name of the word of God, I baptize you in the name of Jesus Christ in the blood of the martyr."

Odessa held her breath while Wallace plunged her backward into the blood. He submerged her beneath the rose-colored water and kept her there for a moment.

Odessa was changed. She was whole again.

She was thrust upward again by the pastor's strong hands, and she blew out her lungful of air, grinning as the bloody water trickled down from her matted hair. Thirty-something church-goers cheered overwhelmingly and shouted saintly things like "Praise Jesus!" and "Hallelujah!" She could hear the rejoicing choir drown out the rumble of the savage weather.

She couldn't have been more divinely overjoyed.

Salvation, at last.

***

The entire ecclesiastical congregation stood outside now, huddled together near a crooked oak's outstretched arms under the cloak of the darkened sky. They were quietly gathered around the mound of espresso-colored dirt where the trough next to the parking lot once was. Ronald was in it now, lumping up the ground.

The sheriff tapped down one last crunchy shovelful of soil. He exhaled a frosty, visible breath of icy January air and leaned the implement against the side of the building. The young men followed suit. They were bundled in thick winter coats now, obscuring the blood-stained outfits beneath.

"Lord, we lay your child down to rest now. He's in your arms, God, rejoicing in the truth and glory of your heavenly presence, Father. We thank you for this day and for your everlasting patience and love for us, Lord."

"Praise Jesus," Nina whispered.

"In your almighty name, we pray, Lord... Amen."

The churchgoers all glanced back up and began to hug each other. They shook hands and started in their separate directions. They knew those were the words with which Pastor Wallace always ended Sunday sermons.

Odessa remained at the grave site as they all scattered to their cars, leaving only Lawrence beside her.

She smiled up at the sky, thrilled the winter squall was about to reprise. As sterling flakes danced around her, she thought about how a blanket of fresh-fallen white powder would soon cover up the stripe of blood up the path. Or how it would smother the churned soil of the trough in a sheet of purity. The earth would be pristine again.

Lawrence dusted a flake from her pink-tinged blonde hair. She smiled at the gesture, her eyes never straying from the burial site.

"We should get you somewhere warm." He was bashful, a caring tone to his voice.

Odessa saw Lawrence in a new light now. He had an attractive jawline, fresh-cut, brassy blond hair, and jarring, cobalt eyes. She had never taken notice of his eyes until now. In all the years she'd been acquainted with him, she wondered if she'd ever really looked at his face. He had always been kind to her. And more than anything, he was a true man of devotion.

How had she never noticed any of this until now?

From the way he was smiling, she could see he was having a similar revelation.

"You live around here, right?" He stepped a little closer, leaving behind two pink bootprints.

She motioned at the trees with a nod. "Just on the other side."

"Can I walk you home?"

Odessa nodded sweetly, stealing another glance at his tender blue eyes.

He held an elbow out. After staring at it briefly, she grasped it. They took a few steps away from the lot through the crunching snow, and Odessa stopped to peek over her shoulder at the grim six-foot-long mound of soil.

For the first time in oh-so-long…

She laughed.

In all the years he'd known Odessa, Lawrence couldn't remember ever having heard her emit so much as a light chuckle before now. He raised an eyebrow quizzically.

She merely replied, "I'm sorry. I couldn't help myself."

ALL THE SAME COLOR
ON THE INSIDE

"It's rag time, Falcon." Harold shuffled his stiff joints down the walkway, trying to adjust his eyes to the searing overhead sun. He grumbled as he picked up the paper at the edge of his shaggy lawn, digging the newsprint out from a patch of overgrowth. His eyes, like summer-sky blues overcast by stormy silver clouds, glared at the interracial couple across the street. They exchanged a kiss in the doorway before the husband, Greg, a uniformed Black man, lumbered to his vehicle. He waved to Harold as a nicety, swishing the sleeve of his police windbreaker, gritted his teeth, and forced a smile. His only experiences with the old codger were negative, but he'd been indoctrinated by idealistic notions like "good guys finish last."

Harold tried to return the expression, but his bobbing, wrinkled face contorted into something more like a sneer. He nodded at Greg, head struggling to crest over his hunched back.

"Goin' to work, huh?" His voice was off-putting, like a witch in a Grimm's fairy tale.

Greg got in, ignoring how obvious the statement was. "Yep. The house doesn't pay for itself."

"Mine's paid off," Harold volunteered, hoping to receive a congratulatory comment from the neighbor he despised. He was deflated when he didn't. "You know…" A facetious grin crept up between the hard lines of his grim, near-translucent face. "Your wife… she's White."

Greg stared at the withered old coot for a moment before muttering with sarcasm, "No shit? Hadn't noticed."

"Well," Harold shrugged and fought back a giggle as if he'd made a full point.

Greg grinned, maintaining composure. "Harold, you know what they say. We're all the same color on the inside. Have a good one, Barry." Greg got in his sleek sedan and slammed the door.

"It's Harry!" Harold hollered, using his rolled newspaper to wave off the car as it sped away, leaving Greg's blonde wife, Sandra, right in his eyeline. She stared for a moment and then shut the door.

Harold's scraggly Maltese yipped up at him from beside his slippers.

"I agree, Falcon. They should stick with their own kind."

Falcon panted up at his aging master, long tufts of unkempt white fur curtained over two ebony eyes, overjoyed by the attention.

"You need to learn how to fetch these damned things for me and start earnin' your keep 'round here." He shook the paper at Falcon, who ached to play.

***

Falcon beat Harold into the house, winding through the maze of dusty "treasures" heaped in treacherous piles throughout the modest single-story interior. Harold shuffled his way into the kitchen past an ancient framed clipping, yellowed through time and aging as poorly as he. The headline read: Rocket Launches, Millner Breaks Connecticut Record and sported a photo of Harold as a young man in his early twenties bursting through finish line tape in a race. His boyish face, unmarred by the devastation of

139

seventy years of hardships and loss, beamed with youthful elasticity and pride.

Harold's shrunken body peered up, the strain of the angle burning his neck. He recalled the days when people called him Rocket because of the breakneck speed he exhibited on the track. Now, the people he worked with to supplement his retirement used the moniker as a comedic antonym because of his leisurely pace any time labor was required, now more a hindrance than a help.

Harold used a leathery, bruised hand to readjust the dust-lined frame, "That's your old man, Falcon. Lifetime ago. You believe that?"

Falcon barked and raced in a tight circle by the pantry door, careful not to ram into any of the towers of heaped clutter.

"Fine. You don't wanna listen to my story, you little shit? You're just like my goddamned real son." He shuffled to the food closet and pulled out a can of dog food. "Ungrateful little bastards, both 'a ya'."

Harold's feeble, age-spotted claw sloshed through the utensil drawer, ultimately locating a grimy can opener. He struggled to clip it to the tin lip and slid the can off the counter onto the floor by accident. It slammed down next to his cotton-colored companion. The scared dog skittered backward into a pile of year-old newspapers and excess dishes stacked near an old fish tank. It hadn't housed anything living in over half a decade.

Harold cackled at the reaction, voice reverberating around the cramped space like an evil dwarf. In a flash, Falcon was back at his heels, licking his chops in anticipation.

Did I feed Falcon yesterday?

...Or the day before?

Harold couldn't recall when the pup's last meal was. Judging by the dog's excitement level, Falcon was starving.

He tried again. This time, the opener caught, crimping a hole into the metal with an audible crunch. He strained to spin the tool's crank, a task he'd never given a second thought to thirty years ago. Menial things were now often exhaustive tasks.

He rotated it, reminiscing about the interview for his first office job five decades prior. The manager, Joe Kowalski, someone he'd later grow to admire, said he was so impressed by Rocket's strong handshake that he'd hired him immediately. He stared at the liver spots beneath the white hair of his knuckles and spun the utensil's wheel. His hand seemed foreign. Ancient.

POP!

The can sounded the completion of its task. He dropped the opener and pressed on one side of the lid to angle the other up enough to grasp it. His feeble fingers missed, and the razor-sharp edge of the can's raw metal sliced through the paper-thin skin of his thumb.

He , flinging the can of meaty gelatinous sauce across the floor. It exploded like a grenade upon impact, spattering the entire kitchen with gravy shrapnel. Falcon descended on the oozing mess seething from the open mouth of the can, mopping up the sloppy brown goo with its snow-white beard as it chowed down.

Harold clutched his wounded hand tight with the other, petrified to view the amount of damage he'd inflicted. He released his fist, and the sliced gash in his finger gushed runny, pulsing sprays of…

Yellow?

In all his years on earth, he'd never seen anything like it. He gasped, fearing the onset of a third heart attack purely from fright. The banging organ thundered in his frail chest. He felt dizzy with fear.

The consistency of the mess seeping from him was akin to tapioca without the pearls. The color was like gooey boil pus, not ruby red like fresh blood.

It wasn't right. None of this was right.

Could it be an infection?

He prayed he was hallucinating the creamy custard-like ichor extruding from the tip of his thumb like extruded icing down the side of a cake. The amount of the substance frothing out of him was equally as terrifying as the hue. The thick matter roiled, d down his shaking, bruised arms like gobs of mud. It drained down his food-stained slacks and onto his blue slippers, gushing harder from the lesion with increasing pressure.

The pain emanating from the gash was excruciating. Harold was alarmed at the inhuman load of gunk churning out from his thumb. The laceration enlarged, splitting the flesh down from the finger pad, tearing the thin skin to the palm, and exposing his muck-covered musculature beneath. It liquefied too. The meat, once capable of an impressive handshake, melted into a thick gelatinous discharge before his eyes.

Harold screamed, drawing the awareness of Falcon, who stood at attention like a loyal, furry soldier. Agony pulsed through Harold as more matter glugged out of the spreading slash, spattering on the floor. Falcon rushed to lap it up greedily.

The rip broadened, and Harold bellowed, "Help me!" as if someone else were nearby who could halt the percolating mess seeping from him.

His fingernail flipped backward and dripped off his hand. Falcon lapped it up with a greedy tongue. It stuck in the matted fur of his face like scotch tape.

The wound widened, shredding a slimy gash up Harold's arm as if something were birthing from the gooey bog inside. The sludge bled onto the ground like gobs of pureed baby food, and starving Falcon lunged on it. Dollops of yellow secretion hailed over stacks of newsprint and bags of moldy refuse.

The pain was unbearable. Harold's devastated form went limp and collapsed into a puddle of expanding ooze spattered across the vintage linoleum. He shuddered in the fattened mess of mustard-colored essence. His essence.

Harold managed a weakened howl of terror mixed with utter confusion. The excruciating rip shredded through his thin, flayed membrane of skin like a fault splitting the land in two during a sizable earthquake. His liver spots were gone now, replaced by tattered, withered strips of flesh extruding marigold matter like a slow-bursting water balloon.

The panicked screams for help stopped after several minutes of sheer agony. The only sounds remaining were birds singing a cheerful tune throughout suburbia outside and the sloppy laps of Falcon's tongue as he enjoyed the rest of his last meal with what remained of his master in peace.

***

Greg squatted down over what was left of Harold's long-dead corpse and the bloated Maltese beside him. A hoard of flies swarmed them both, and maggots writhed in Falcon's mouth and along his stained arms, crusted in something a putrid buttery shade of yellow.

What survived of the old man wasn't much. He couldn't determine what caused the geezer to be annihilated in such a hideous fashion.

Greg covered his face with a swishing sleeve of his uniform. He hadn't seen the wrinkly senior citizen in at least three weeks. If not for the welfare check called in by another nosy neighbor, Greg would have gone a year without the safety of the racist windbag ever crossing his mind. He stared into the destroyed, rigored body of the mangled, wormy elder. The pus-colored matter had caked in every cranny of his neighbor's hardened, putrefied cavities.

Greg thought about those last words he'd uttered to the old man a month ago and how wrong they might have been.

Maybe we aren't all the same color on the inside after all.

That thought and Harold's rancid decomposition made Greg crack a smile. He choked it back and stood up over the gruesome scene, feigning reverence for what remained of the old man.

SECONDHAND KISS

"Okay. Fair point about the Mayan culture. I think I see where you're coming from as far as the sacrificial aspect goes. So, let me ask you a follow-up question then." Smoke crept out from between Sandra's plump lips as she politely passed the joint, her soothing voice low from the deep inhalation. "Do you believe in God?"

Her eyes darted wildly, scanning all of the holiday commotion below.

As Thomas McGregor stared at those hazel irises, ones that seemed to hold all the colors of the cosmos, he knew that he, in fact, did. He sensed that only someone - or something - as omniscient and powerful as God would be capable of producing a creature as flawless as the celestial being before him.

She leaned further over the rooftop rails, studying the raucous people below, prancing through the streets of New Haven in Halloween costumes requiring varying efforts. Her auburn locks fluttered in the chilled, briny breeze as she locked her sights on a couple. Their hands were clasped in affection. The male was dressed like a ghoul in a tattered cape, the woman a slutty angel.

Yes, he was certain of it. Some ultimate power vigorously gathered every one of those freckles, speckled across her supple cheeks like some intricate stelliform constellation. Some deity chose her delicate nose, puffy lips, and perfectly angled collarbones, knowing they would all work together to form the most magnetizing combination. It was unfathomable for such angelic features and sublime, feminine curves to ever be assembled at random. She was perfection.

He also imagined the one that created her from the most idyllic materials to be a God capable of massive cruelty. Savage enough to forge a creature whose utterance of Thomas's name from her honeyed lips halted time. The sound of her saccharine-sweet voice was capable of stranding him in a frozen moment like this, invaded by lust and utterly painful yearning. Only an inhuman entity could've chosen two kaleidoscopic vortexes straight from the night sky as eyes for her luminous face and then, with those same ruthlessly unkind hands, haphazardly jammed dirt-brown ones into the deep-set sockets behind his prescription glasses. In the hours since they'd met, he felt an insatiable longing for her.

Her hands pressed down on the rail. He fantasized about their touch. How could the seraphic power involved in the sculpting of hers, so dainty and unmarred, have also constructed the two trembling, sweating hands that now pinched his smoldering joint?

Yes. He believed in God. That terrible, cruel God that would place someone so out of his league right there before him. He was just an indebted college student with nothing to offer but love.

He clasped the joint awkwardly and drew it to his lips with his trembling hand. He tried to dismiss it as the brisk night air sending a shiver through him, but he knew deep down that it was her making his hand quiver. He savored a puff. The paper wrap sizzled. He prolonged the deep, aromatic inhalation, delighting in the notion that his lips had just touched something hers had, like some sort of secondhand kiss.

The icy air was filled with the whoops and howls and bellows of a bustling college town that sprang to life at night. And one even more alive on Halloween. The students were cutting loose and bar-hopping along the downtown green. Thomas wondered what it would be like to be like one of those below them. Popular. Charismatic. Included in group activities. Anonymous, thanks to some cheap rubber mask.

Instead, Tom found himself racked with anxiety. He felt as if he was hurtling indefinitely through space. No real remaining family or close friendships. No major. Little direction. Little drive. A mounting pile of tuition and textbook bills. Craving this one romantic connection before him that was so close and, simultaneously, light years away.

Sandra was the first girl he'd conversed with, and I mean really conversed with on a deeper level, in so long. It was only a matter of time before she wised up and realized she belonged down there, walking the colorful crosswalks, frolicking amid a gaggle of other gorgeous twenty-somethings flaunting her perfect body in some whoreish costume along the Black Lives Matter asphalt mural on that green. He knew in his bones that she didn't belong up here with him, hidden from the world like some sad, dark secret.

"Well? Do you?" Sandra's dreamlike voice snapped him back into the moment, almost as if the suspended second hand of the stuck clock started ticking again.

He'd almost forgotten the question, lost in her eyes. Those dazzling eyes that glittered in the lights of the city. After a puff, he nodded, returning rapidly from being so deeply submerged in contemplation that he could get 'the bends.'

"Yeah, I do." Thomas let the smoke fill his lungs. "Not in the way people like the Mayans did. But, yeah, I was raised with religious values. I don't know how much of my belief structure has just been indoctrinated during my formative years and how much I still believe if I take a solid look at all of the evidence. And I don't know if any particular religion has gotten it 'right,' so to speak, but yeah, I think I do believe. I just think God might be a sadist."

Sandra's laugh was genuine, melting him like ice cream on a scorching sidewalk. Blood coursed through his temples as her gaze caressed him, her expression warm and bright.

"That's dark." She took another drag and handed the joint back, adding, "How so?"

Thomas laughed, collecting scattered, straying thoughts with haste. Once he was intoxicated, he feared he'd verbally meander without ever making a real point. What he uttered was vague and less-than-perspicacious. "Have you even read the Bible?"

"Which one? There are a lot of 'em."

"True. I guess I am referring to, like, the King James Version."

"Oh." She drank in the merriment of another group on the sidewalk, all bee-lining towards the assaulting bass and radiant lights emitted by the neon-rimmed bar on the corner. Two men were in nearly matching Victorian vampire garb. One girl was a sexy cat in a tiny fur-lined outfit that exposed her toned, fish-netted thighs and a straggler in a red-and-green Freddy-esque sweater dress, her bountiful cleavage bulging through slashes. "So that's the God you're referring to? The so-called Christian God?"

"Well, I obviously can't say if He's that, exactly."

"He?" She grinned, eyes sparkling in the brilliant tungsten lights of the five-level parking garage a block away.

"He... or she." He stood. "Or it. Or they/them, I don't fucking know."

Even though they'd only met this afternoon, Thomas was taken by her. He felt like his presence was blessed by this striking astronomy major who miraculously teleported into his life, invading his every thought ever since.

She was something special.

He knew, if granted even the most tenuous opportunity, he'd worship her in the holiest of ways. Thomas had given her his number earlier in the hallway of the literary arts building, where they'd struck up a conversation. It was kismet. He offered to give her a tour of the campus, knowing she'd never use it. He was flummoxed when he received the first text from her, only hours later as he slurped down a bowl of beef Ramen. The sound of the text was euphoric. And now, after a few hours on a rooftop spent philosophizing about a variety of topics and motifs, it was as if he'd known her for multiple lifetimes.

He wondered if she could hear the sound of his heart slamming out of his rib cage, thumping clumsily against the walls of his chest. Or if she sensed the tingling in his belly and the yearning in his soul every time he looked at her.

"Well, first—" Thomas took another drag and erupted into a violent coughing fit. He could already feel the effects of the first hit, slowly altering his perception. The dispensary goods were so strong, and he was still so new to smoking it. It had only recently become legal, and Thomas wasn't one to break the law, despite being goaded and chided by his sparse friends over the years to do so.

"You alright?" Sandra's intense eyes locked on him. Her playful grin was like an arrow shot straight through his burning throat. "Do I need to give you mouth-to-mouth?"

Oh God, YES, he thought, his mouth unable to utter a single sound.

He imagined that sight: Her innocent, luminous face poised over his as he struggled for breath on the ground. Her long, wavy hair dripped like a curtain of lustrous raspberry sun tea, offering full seclusion. That divine mouth pressed to his, intimately invigorating him with ethereal breaths of vital air.

Wait, was this a hint? Was she... flirting with him? His heart leaped at the implication. Blood surged between his legs, rendering him lightheaded, wincing about the stiffness and throbbing beneath his jeans.

He wished he was dying. Wished his heart would stop pumping blood altogether so it would halt the rigidity that would soon be undeniably noticeable and certainly humiliating.

He wanted to kiss her now, to flip their budding friendship like a coin, letting it land wherever it belonged. He wished the weed had given him some courage, but it only seemed to dilate time. He felt like the moments between his responses —moments like this — were, instead, hours. Hours lost in thought. Lost in her stunning gaze. Hours frozen like a Jedi in carbonite.

Agonizingly frozen, his mind screamed for him to seize the moment. A simple task and, yet, the hardest thing he'd ever done.

His body wouldn't budge.

And he hated himself for it.

Sandra arose, and the crushing weight of reality hit him as the opportunity slipped away.

"You good?" She smiled coyly and meandered to another rail, gazing with vibrant, glittering irises at clusters of drab, colorless buildings in downtown New Haven. Theirs, a colonial-era citadel overlooking a modern-day kingdom. The palatial buildings of the campus stood like castles. Imposing, broad, and timeworn. Massive stone structures over three hundred years old that are taken for granted by all the bourgeois Ivy League students doling out over-inflated admissions.

Her cosmological eyes flit across the landscape like a queen lording from a castle spire. By day, the dense throngs of trees were alive, bounding with a full spectrum of fiery hues. Terracotta, umber, garnet, and marigold leaves peppered the scenic vista: a yearly explosion of color before leaves trembled from their boughs, leaving abandoned skeletal trunks to scrape thin fingers of bark across the sky in their stead. By night, however, the colors were muted by darkness, illuminated in patches by street lamps and the full orb of the milk-white moon, itself an ominous statement piece amid a charcoal sky laden with sooty clouds.

Sandra giggled, and the bright sound formed a smile on Tom's face.

"What?" Tom giggled, too, the weed hitting him now like a concussive brick to the head.

"I don't know. I guess it's just a little funny that you said you believed in God but have yet to elaborate."

She was right. He was so lost in thought, so stoned, and so drunk on her beauty that he'd completely lost sight of the question again. "I think there's something out there. The universe is so vast, possibly infinite. I mean, I don't need to tell you that. You're majoring in it. But it's clear we've only just discovered a tiny fraction of it."

"You say 'we' like humans are the only beings that matter."

"I mean, who knows what the galaxy holds? I don't necessarily believe we're the only things out there. That would be arrogant."

"Well, the human race usually is." Her tone was wistful and melancholy.

"No shit. Anything could be out there. But as far as God goes, to answer your question, I guess I don't think He is, like, what most Americans think He is, which is that."

Thomas pointed down to a frat boy in a white robe, long white wig, and a shepherd's hook racing toward his fraternity brethren. The men hollered loudly, and one, dressed as a buff police officer, his biceps choked by the rolled-up sleeves on the costume, spoke. His voice carried. "You look so stupid."

"You're just jealous." The frat boy screamed like a wolf howling into the night, "Because I'm God among men!"

Thomas snickered. "I don't think there's any chance that God is like some Caucasian dude in an oversized, sloppy robe."

"That is something I never understood," Sandra interjected, her tone serious. "Humans calling God a male. On Earth, females are the almost sole creators of brand-new, vital matter. They are the bringers of new life. The only reason for their continued existence is because women have continued to bear more slightly askew copies of them for centuries. They're nurturers and creators. Not destroyers. They're blind architects with surprise blueprints for every future construction project."

"Whoa." Thomas smirked, struggling to keep up, but her words and notions started to breeze over his ballooning head.

"I know what Gods really are," she continued. Her calm, soothing voice penetrated his ears through the hushed fog of inebriation. "They're neither woman nor man and bear no earthly resemblance whatsoever to either."

He snorted, giggling hard, trying to squelch the desire for full-on laughter. It wasn't funny, but Sandra's grave tone elicited a reaction of nervous hilarity in his high, twenty-year-old mind. He composed himself. "Androgynous polytheism. I can get behind that."

"Astrophysical elders, ones that existed before time as you understand it." She took another long drag and handed the minuscule remainder of the cannabis back to him.

Thomas licked his thumb and index fingers and suffocated the cherry, stashing the remnant behind his ear. "Crazy." His simple reply was flippant. Her theories made less sense the more the sativa raged. He bumbled into a hazy digression. "I find it amazing that there are, like, seven billion people, and maybe countless other unexplored planets in this, probably limitless, galaxy and, yet, somehow, we sometimes manage to still be utterly... alone. We're surrounded by this," he swirled his hands in passionate illustration, "swarm of life around us, and, yet, we're empty."

"I know that feeling all too well." Despair seeped from her words, expression despondent.

"How on Earth could someone as... spectacular as you ever be lonely? What an honest-to-God travesty." He mused, astonished to hear the words gush from his mouth without a filter.

"I've lived in isolation longer than you can possibly imagine, Thomas."

He stared quizzically, brown eyes glued to her moon-kissed face. "Why? You move around a lot?"

He pictured childhood Sandra as an Army brat, constantly packing and unpacking. Auditioning for new cliques at every school. Then he imagined a home-schooled Sandra with well-meaning nomadic parents, showing her the natural wonders of the country from an airstream. He didn't want to pry and instead waited patiently for whatever scraps she was willing to feed him about her past.

She managed a slight, sad smile. "Oh, yes, constantly traveling. I reach out all the time, but every time, no matter what, I just end up starting up all alone again somewhere else."

"That breaks my heart." He uttered with melancholic reverence.

"It's draining." She sighed and stared out at the people, like ants, scrawled across the campus below. "But I've made friends all over."

"Must be nice. I rarely travel." He stared off, unable to see the nearby Long Island Sound through the cluster of aging buildings but smelling its faint waft of seaweed and salt in the autumn air just the same.

"Would you like to?"

"Sure. Hell, I've never even been south of Jersey." He grinned a little wider. "I'd love to go far from here. See it all."

Her gaze locked on him, her voice tinged with urgency. "Let's go tonight. Wherever you want to go."

He laughed at the incredulity. "Funny, I hadn't pegged you as some kinda trust fund baby with a private jet." He snickered. "But then again, this is an Ivy—"

"No jet. You name the place, and I'll take you there." She was earnest, hopeful.

"Anywhere?" He laughed, threw his hands upward playfully, and scoffed. "Sure, uh, how about the Antrim Coast? Got some very distant relatives there."

"Oooh. Northern Ireland." She grinned. "Exquisite. Excellent choice."

"You've been?"

"Many, many times." Her tone was convincing, which made it harder for Thomas to control his laughter. "It's gorgeous there this time of year. It's raining there right now. Magnificent views. You've never seen grass so green in your life." Her hands began moving excitedly, illustrating a vast rolling landscape. "Waves of emerald mile-after-rolling-mile. You'll love it, Thomas."

Thomas erupted in an unflattering honk of laughter followed by the timid point of his index finger. "Girl, you are so hiiiiigh."

"Perhaps." She stepped to him. The dimples in her cheeks grew deeper upon approach. "Please come with me." Her voice was hungry, pleading.

They were touching. Body to body, their dewy clothes melded. The air was electric, offering a zing of excitement to his eager flesh. His heart banged like an unbalanced washing machine, smashing swiftly like a bouncing ball, clattering against the bones in his chest.

"I'm so lonely, Thomas." Shimmering tears plunged down her glistening, freckle-smattered cheeks, voice full of ache, oozing pain.

The longing and sorrow dripping from her words crushed down on him like a weight from above. He desired to strike those words permanently from her vocabulary. Now that she had finally met him, Thomas vowed to remedy that.

"You're not alone," he said, voice a hushed whisper.

But it wasn't true.

He didn't dare to break his gaze into her arresting eyes, those dizzying galactic kaleidoscopes of silver, blue, and green hues alight from the moon's brilliant beam. He saw the reflection of his awkward, black frames in each, peppering dulled specks of darkness through the array of colors.

"Please," she begged, tears roiling like running brooks. "Please, Thomas, I would do anything to not be so alone."

Those words were the last Thomas would ever hear...

On this planet or on any other.

I would do anything to not be so alone.

He caressed her bottom lip with his thumb, the force parting them. Then he kissed her.

And she kissed back. Eagerly.

She returned his affection with a force unlike any earthly emotion or touch he'd ever experienced. In a moment, everything began to shift. The collegiate woman before him proved illusory. His world was upended.

Intense passion gave way to a tidal wave of morose misery, blanketing him like a drowning man caught in the middle of a natural disaster. Panicked anxiety illuminated the neural network spider-webbed through his befuddled brain. The astronomical event extended far beyond the scope of Thomas's reality.

The hazel wonderlands that once were her irises now sat barren and empty. Two frosted white orbs fixed within her changing face. The touch of her flesh burned him, but he was powerless to pull away. Their pressed epidermal layers began a painful fusion, and through it, he understood Sandra's emotions. He understood the painful crushing of eons of longing, searching simply for a kindred soul within the icy vastness of the universe.

His eyes were the first to go, bursting violently in their deep-set sockets like smashed grapes, spattering hot, watery, crimson fluid against the interior of his glasses. The haze of the joint wore off quickly, and white-hot pain shot through him as his nerves and tendons snapped like abused ruddy guitar strings. His bones shattered brutally, grinding together within his loosening skin. His screaming face drooped like putty with a malleability that suggested there was no elastic collagen remaining in his deteriorating frame.

Tom's chest shuddered. One at a time, his ribs cracked and crumbled. Concave where they once sat convex, snapping like wishbones with audible cracks. His muscles were pulverized as if battered to liquid form by a mallet. His screams soaked into the void of her mouth between the flawless lips that offered his final and most brutal act of intimacy.

The bones in his lower legs shattered and snapped like glow sticks. His body convulsed as his fragmented tibias and fibulas were ground into grievous bundles of anatomical confusion. His consciousness remained painfully intact as his body came apart at the seams.

As the pain gave way to a bewildering mental evolution, Thomas began to comprehend the previously unfathomable immensity of the universe and its complex weave of galactic interconnectivity.

He was cognizant of the insignificance of humans. Undeserved egos and narcissism running rampant, like lethal plagues foreshadowing the eventual demise of their race, their arrogance laughable in the grand scheme. Mere ants in perspective to physically tangible beings on other planets, both in size and importance.

A surge of mind-bending concepts injected his consciousness like a needle full of pure heroin, overloading his remaining senses as the entity, once called Sandra, enveloped him.

Her once-delicate maw was now an impossibly cavernous monstrosity. She inhaled, absorbing him into a cosmic cloud of violet and cerulean gasses oozing from between two gaping jaws.

As swift as it began, the searing pain subsided, and Thomas's body was gone. He was inside of her — understanding Sandra wasn't a her at all. This thing, this essence — it was something else altogether.

It was both God and slave. It was a vital force of substantial magnitude. All genders and species bleeding together at once. It was an ancient, intergalactic existence. An elder presence of exceptional age and wisdom.

…And of considerable sadness.

Forsaken and boundaryless, it was bursting with curiosity. It force-fed on Thomas's body in a cleanup effort. The force was wise enough not to leave loose ends dangling, even on a planet as inconsequential as Earth.

The mortal momentarily satiated the entity's need for connection, though it was not nearly enough. Thomas's flesh was now dissolved, vanishing with the swirling gasses, rising back into the ether from which it appeared a week ago, leaving nothing behind but marijuana ash and a puddle of dark, viscous blood and ichor seeping into the gravel on the dormitory rooftop.

Thomas was no longer Thomas. His soul was a part of something bigger now. Melded as one with the immortal force now, and the others consumed before him. Together, they roamed the skies to make one more earthly visit before returning to the infinite cosmological outer depths of space, from which it originated.

A morphed form of Tom's consciousness remained, just for a few more blissful moments. His awareness lasted long enough for him to experience the damp patter of Northern Irish rain rushing through him, through them, as they drifted overhead like a galactic drone, sweeping through miles of the Antrim Coast. The entity patiently allowed him to drink in the crystal-clear view of the defunct, crumbling castles followed by an expansive stretch of breathtaking emerald grass, richer and more vivid than anything he'd ever seen with his long-gone mortal eyes.

What remained of Thomas soaked up swaying Elysian fields of vibrant, lush greenery, just as he'd been promised, before the melded entity began the expansive drift to what it considered home. The idyllic view was a partially self-serving parting gift to Tom from the entity to express its gratitude for the brief but genuine companionship.

Thomas was now one with the looming deity, amalgamated with the countless others before him, their mortal existences each eternally altered forever by a secondhand kiss.

Swirling through the cosmos, hurtling through space, it pondered where it might travel next and what form it might take as it existed infinitely, tainted by a depressive fog of solitude, craving even the most fleeting, destructive taste of companionship to pass the time on a halted clock, stranded and victim to the immensity of eternity.

TAKE A BREATH

I jolt in my seat. Blood pounds through my graying temples. My heart thumps. The blast of the horn behind me sends an icy shiver across my skin. My preoccupied mind failed to register the green light above. I smash the gas, jerking my Subaru into motion, hurtling myself through the intersection. As I lurch through the signal, my distracted mind is stuck on the tone of Mr. Carey's voice as he said the words, "Pack your things. You're done."

Shit-canned.

I'm part of the jobless masses talked about on the evening news. I'll have to fight for something new, something paying notably less. Or worse, go on unemployment. I shudder at the thought of all the online forms. The arguing. The government bureaucracy. The smile fading from

169

the attractive cashier's face as I hand over my EBT card to charge a block of cheddar. I imagine myself weeks from now choking back tears of frustration with a mouth full of shitty grilled-cheese sandwich as I read another rejection letter after a promising interview.

We regret to inform you…

That's always how it starts, isn't it?

"We regret to inform you, Mr. Alexander, that we wish to go in a different direction for the position."

They won't want this chump. I'm just some jerk-off who's given nine years to a company that cut me like a mat on a dog's ass the first time I made a mistake. Or maybe it'll go well.

"May we call your previous employer for a reference, Lawrence?"

I laugh. That'll go over like a lead balloon.

I can hear Mr. Carey's voice laughing into the phone now: "Yeah, Larry flew under the radar and was otherwise the human version of cellophane til he embarrassed himself in the end—"

Maybe I'll make the big time with Rusty. For a moment, it seems possible. If I were to rededicate my body, surfing for a living might not be a pipe dream. They say 10,000 hours is enough to make one a master at anything. I've certainly put in close to that amount of beach time through the years. And my schedule just opened up... wide.

Right now, the serotonin dump from riding a wave might be the only thing I have to live for.

Sarah would have laughed at the outrageous concept of me going "pro" at any sport. She was unflinchingly supportive but a belly laugh would've been her knee-jerk reaction if I said it out loud. Followed by active, desperate backpedaling to spare my feelings, ending with a speech about how I can do anything I put my mind to.

Oh, Sarah...

An overwhelming wave of tension and panic washes over me. The empty passenger seat burns a hole in my soul.

Take a breath.

And I do.

I pull off Matunuck Beach Road and park on the brush-lined roadside. After an hour and change, I'm here: A secret spot tucked away on the Rhode Island Shoreline behind a dense thicket of foliage with a great point break known only to a handful of serious New England surfers, dubbed Siren's Cove.

Despite the sluggish string of traffic outside of Mystic, I arrive at my favorite time of day: just before sunset. I love watching that flaming ball of light dive down below the waves from atop Rusty.

I plunk my wallet and keys into the glove box and lug myself out of the car. As I stretch, my back cracks like a glow stick, and I holler the groan of someone being tortured in a medieval device.

Time to get to work.

Ugh, the irony.

I pop the alligator buckles on the roof rack and release Rusty from its clutches. The foam and fiberglass bounce back beneath the loosened nylon bands like the board's been holding his breath. I toss the straps on the box of cleaned-out office supplies in the back seat. Despair washes over me as I see nine forfeited years lumped between cardboard walls. Glancing at my employee badge makes me ill.

The tightness in my chest chokes the air from my lungs. I'm experiencing another panic attack. Oh God, not another one. I force my own body to drag air in. Breathing no longer feels automatic.

Take a breath.

And I do.

I rub Rusty's fiberglass surface with a wax bar and snatch up the spring suit rumpled in a rubbery pile in the back. Its charcoal-colored interior is still lined with grit, causing a zing of excitement as I slide my legs into it. I've missed the feel of sand against my bare skin.

I stuff myself in, aware of how much excess weight I packed on due to the sedentary job, the drinking, and my recent 'depressive episode' (as my counselor calls it.)

I reach in through the window and produce a chrome flask. Why'd you have to go and cause this mess, little fella? We were friends. I take a swig. The cheap vodka burns, but I know the confidence I'll get will satisfy.

Hell, one more swig won't hurt…

I lob the metal container back inside and clutch Rusty's hardened shell tight against me, jammed painfully deep in my armpit. I coil the leash and take off through the thicket, careful not to smack Rusty's fins. Despite the whipping Rhode Island winds slapping me, I still can't seem to gasp enough air. The humidity wraps around my face like a sopping towel.

I trudge down the narrow, secluded path, snaking through thin trees until it opens up to the rocky Block Island Sound. I should be grateful for so many things in this picturesque moment. Instead, the world feels like it's collapsing, burying me in a pile of rubble too heavy to escape.

A seagull cries out, snapping me from the dark whirlwind of panic and into the crisp spring moment. A sideways blast of chilling air ruffles through my curly hair, and my once-hot, pumping blood is now replaced with blended iced coffee-like slurry. In my stomach, the alcohol lands like a hot missile being detonated in a barren, arid field.

Kaboom.

The warm aftershock of the blast radiates, and the tingle of inebriation hits. The rapid change in temperature is unsettling. A throbbing sensation clatters through my head, and I'm slammed with a wave of vertigo. Another panic attack is looming right around the corner. I know it.

Or perhaps I'll get lucky, and it'll be another full-fledged breakdown.

Spin the roulette wheel, Larry. Let's see what humiliating reaction the ball lands on.

No. My counselor reprimanded me for this sort of spiraling.

Remember what she said:

Take a breath.

And I do.

As I struggle to control my thoughts, I focus and take in a lungful of salty ocean air with a slow cigarette-like drag until I'm at the water's edge. I kick off my flip-flops and work my muscles, lunging and stretching, focusing on the low tide. The view before me is like an oil painting, rich with turquoise and blue hues, punctuated by expansive crests of bubbly white foam.

To my surprise, even with large, wild waves, I have my pick of any spot here. Though this rock-laden area is a hidden gem, many are still aware it exists. Still, I've never seen this place so empty, especially during low tide.

About 150 yards away, an enticing set rushes forth just beyond an outcropping of massive rocks. From here, the waves look deceptively modest, but I know from their height and heaviness, as well as from the way they're breaking, that they're monumental. They're a little sloppy from parallel-gusting side winds, but they're big.

Eight feet? Maybe ten?

I eye the area behind the outcropping and opt to save my strength for the gigantic waves themselves. Perhaps I can use the force of the nearby channel to help carry me out to conserve some energy. The paralyzing tide whooshes past my ankles, swells to my calves, and snaps me from my focused calculations.

The cold water is arresting.

There's still time to turn back.

But where would I go? Home? To an average apartment infused with haunting reminders of her? Or to work? Pffft. Thanks to the fermented potato juice in my Outback, I'm no longer welcome there.

Focus, Larry.

The chilling current beckons me. I summon the courage to force myself in. I still can't believe I'm alone. Normally, there are at least some surfers here, straddling boards like upright neoprene-clad seals, vying for the best spot in the rotation.

But not today.

Is this an omen or much-needed luck? Maybe it's because it's a Wednesday. After all, most people are still at work. They have jobs.

Ugh, that's depressing.

I sigh at the thought of being penniless and unemployed on top of my crushing aimlessness since Sarah. I've had my fill of desolation these last two months. If she were here, she'd plunk down her foam-covered longboard and goad me in with that playful, teasing tone. She'd whirl her ankle leash around like some cowboy's lasso and pretend to yank me in the bubbling surf like a helpless steer.

It's never the ones you'd expect, they say.

That hidden, unadulterated sadness can seat itself behind a genuine smile, attaching like some insidious cancer, subtly wasting its once-happy host to a hollow, empty shell.

It's never the ones you'd expect.

I look at the sky as if my decades of Catholic tone-deaf humming on my knees and drowsy sermons about Hell as punishment for suicide never happened. I scan for some semblance of Sarah's face in the billowing puff balls rolling high overhead. Instead, ominous, color-bereft pockets of seaweed-scented moisture loom. I wonder if these sudden pangs of melancholy will ever leave for me.

Take a breath, Larry.

And I do.

After strapping the leash to my ankle, Rusty and I make our way out into the murky waters like inseparable old friends. Water sloshes loudly around me like kids splashing joyfully in a bathtub.

Don't think about bathtubs...

This is the first time that the loud, crashing sound of the waves doesn't drown out the megaphone volume of my thoughts, but still, I wade deeper until the water is sloshing around my waist. The ocean feels like chaos. I hurl myself atop Rusty's fiberglass surface harder than

I should've. The awkward mounting sends a shock wave of pain through my chest. I'm ashamed of the amateur move.

Dammit, focus, Larry.

Ugh, I'm getting too heavy for this board.

I paddle out toward the continuous sets in the distance until I reach the impact zone. Despite using the energy of the channel, I'm still feeling out of breath, and my shoulders sting from paddling through the churning waters. I bob above a long sand bar parallel with the choppy swells. I settle myself and take a mental note of the geography of the mammoth rocks in the area. The setting sun is washing the sky with a rosy, dusky hue of pink, and the only things out here in the deeper waters with me are the squawking gulls and whatever lurks in the water below me.

This next wave's got my name all over it.

I squint at the wave beside me, lower myself to my belly, and concentrate. Facing the empty, rocky shoreline, I swim in overdrive, shoving huge handfuls of foamy saltwater behind me. I question if I've chosen the right time to paddle. I wonder if I'm too deep in the pocket and will just end up getting tossed.

The wave swells beneath Rusty, lifting us both up like the giant hand of Poseidon. For a second, I'm weightless. In this momentary limbo,

I experience a sudden pulse of panic. No matter how many times I'm in surf this large, this challenging, there is always a gut-wrenching tinge of terror, like I'm about to fall from a violent height. The wave surges upward with raw, natural power, and the ocean hurls me back toward dry land like it's rejecting me.

Operating on pure muscle memory, I pop up on Rusty. I raise my body and cut the water with the subtle pressure of my feet. I cruise along the bottom edge of the wave toward the rock break with agile precision, careful not to clip any of them. It would be easy to do and dangerous, especially in this low tide. The exhilarating rush of chemicals flooding my brain reminds me how much this sport has been my saving grace for decades.

Rusty's back fins slice through the liquid like a hot knife through butter as we glide smoothly across the trough. The wave is breaking behind me, and I coast below it with careless abandon. It's the first time I have felt even a moment of peace since Sarah.

Don't think about Sarah. This is not the time or the place—

My thoughts are cut short as Rusty's fin slams against something rigid beneath the surface. I lose my balance with the abrupt halt of the momentum, and I'm propelled forward, slamming my knee hard on the face of an unforgiving rock. Pain rings out, and I can detect that the startling crunch my knee made is going to be a problem. I gather myself, take a deep breath, and fling my salty mop of hair out of my eyes. As I tread water, every kick sends a sharp, agonizing ache up through my aging body. I probably tore something again. This is the last thing I need: another knee surgery with no job and no company health insurance.

I wade for another moment, judging whether I can continue with this excruciating pain. It hurts, but I'll live. Rusty floats behind me on his springy leash, tethered like a brownish-red shadow. I can sense anger and frustration bubbling up from my vodka-coated belly and into my skull like a crock of hot soup boiling over. I let out a furious growl at my failing body and struggle to slip back on top of my board.

Get back out there this instant, Larry.

Without a rest, I paddle back out toward the same spot. I don't want to miss my chance and have to wait out a lull. A tinge of lavender starts to stain the sunset, and there are only a few more opportunities before the sun drops for the day. The strong current of the nearby channel beckons me like a reaper's index finger, and I use that force and my pent-up fury to make it back with haste. The salty brine rushes past the bare flesh of my limbs as I float, patiently waiting for the next wave. They're constant today, operating like a well-oiled machine in perfect rhythmic time with itself. The ocean lowers and then raises me like an exhilarating, hydraulic carnival ride.

It's time.

I paddle toward the break with every ounce of energy within me. I rise with the powerful wave and bat the water with enough force to propel me forward, locking into the momentum.

I hear a sound. It seems familiar, cooing softly to my left. I whip my head to look, but something dark and large dips back below the churning surface before I can get a good look.

What was that? A seal?

My gaze returns, and my hands flatten onto Rusty. I push up, swing my feet into position, and thrust myself up.

Searing pain rips up through my leg, and my injured knee buckles hard. I careen through the air, weightless once again. I wipe out mercilessly on an angular boulder that the rushing tide has just unveiled below. Trying to catch my fall, my left arm contorts unnaturally under the crashing force of my body. My chin smashes down into the unforgiving stone next. My jaw cracks forcefully and my molars gouge deep tears straight through my tongue. I taste coppery blood immediately.

An anguishing pain pounds through my mouth and forearm. As the wave rushes past, I suck in a deep breath of air. I'm shaking in shock and disbelief. I use my right arm to try to pull Rusty back toward me, but a new, even more colossal wave surges forth. With the rubber leash in hand, I grip it tightly as the water begins to whisk me off the rock. Rusty peels downward with the tether, tearing away from a great height. I look up in time to witness Rusty's hardened body diving down an uninterrupted path straight at me like a kamikaze pilot. He unflinchingly mangles my face in one deeply brutal instant. A deafening thwap rings out through my skull as the nose of the stout fiberglass board slams into my eye socket with all the gruesome force it can muster, banging me backward onto another jagged boulder.

The wave envelops me now, and I'm tumbling, disoriented through a turbulent mess of water and bubbles, tangled in Rusty's leash. Beneath the churning surface, I cling to the underside of the slippery board with all my might. The power of the next gargantuan wave sends me hurtling spine-first into another boulder, causing me to release my grip on it. The upward-shooting force of the buoyant board sends the unyielding material of Rusty's hardened fins slicing effortlessly through the soft flesh of my face.

Red. That's all I'm enveloped by.

A gushing stream of blood muddies the water around me, spewing forth from my gashed cheek and socket. My remaining vision and depth perception are skewed, and terror settles in as I realize that I've gone blind in my right eye.

No, God, no.

I want to go back.

Control+Alt+Delete.

Still, the ocean rages on. It feels like war. I'm mutilated on the battlefield as this combative force wages on around me, unsympathetic to the trauma it has just inflicted upon my body.

I crave the urge to palpate my face to find out if my eye is still in its socket, but my working arm is too busy flapping wildly. It's fight or flight time, and bone-chilling panic begins to flood my every muscle. Briny saltwater stings my open wounds like white-hot coals as the water thrashes me against the rocks again. Through the murk and bubbles, all I can see is red.

Just like when I opened the bathroom door.

Sarah lay there, carved up in the tub in our apartment, pale legs akimbo over the side. Her head was fully submerged beneath the glassy surface of the tepid, scarlet water. She was still. It was a level of stillness I'd never witnessed before.

Is this a nightmare? I'm desperate to wake up.

I'm thrust again under the surface by the next ceaseless wave. Deafening crimson water gurgles around my hemorrhaging head, agitated by my own panicked thrashing. I'm choking on ocean water and blood, and I can't hold in any air with this grisly, gaping laceration in my cheek.

My skull pounds, and the low, throbbing rush of fluid coursing through my brain roars louder as I choke violently.

Again, I hear the strange sounds, the loving soft gurgling through the water like a lullaby. The sound has a chilling familiarity, but I can't quite place it.

Bleakly-lit bubbles through the red-green water trail above me as I'm wrenched down into the ocean's inky black depths. Fresh air seems so impossibly far away.

I paddle hard with my intact right arm, but I'm undeniably disoriented. A wave catches Rusty and jerks me through the water by my tethered leash. I can't catch a single gulp of oxygen.

The singing grows louder, pounding in my brain now like an amplifier with the bass cranked. I know the tune, but I still can't place it. It sounds like something Sarah used to hum to me when I was down with the flu.

In fact, it sounds just like Sarah when I think about it…

My salt-filled sinuses burn, and I'm starting to suffocate slowly, just a few mere feet beneath the rippling surface, trembling in agony. I struggle, eyes locked on the light beams above.

I break through and gasp a sweet lungful of humid air with everything in me. My efforts have led me astray as the choppy swells and panicked flailing have sent me whirling further from shore. I flail my burning limb and gag on seawater as I scream out for help. No one is near enough in this aquatic Hell to be aware of my existence. The pain in my broken arm increases to a nauseating level as the ocean tosses me about. I lurch toward Rusty, who remains completely unscathed and oblivious to the brutality that has just occurred. If I can manage my way atop him, I'll be buoyant. I'll be able to catch my breath. I'll be able to float back to shore.

Before my hands can find purchase on the glossy board, Rusty jets away from me, and another huge wave bears down overhead, pushing me deep underwater. Serrated knife-like pains stab through the middle of my knee every time I kick. The liquid surges harder, dragging me into the massive rocks littering the ocean floor again. My blood drags like a chem trail as I'm whisked away with the tide. I struggle to find the urge within me to continue to fight through the agonizing pain and overwhelming exhaustion.

I'm under for too long this time. My lungs are constricting in the suffocating embrace of the ocean's watery arms. The surface is so dishearteningly distant now. Perhaps it's because of my flawed depth perception. Or possibly the tide is so forceful that it all really is as far away as it appears. I am drifting wide-eyed and wounded through the murk.

Like Sarah…

Her eyes were open. She stared at me through the stained glass-like water with no life behind those chillingly still eyes. Gone was her very essence of being. The glinting razor sat on the tile floor beside us as I begged her to wake up.

But she never would again.

Hysteria floods me as I scramble up, entombed by liquid. This asphyxiation is making me dizzy, and my dimming vision blurs further. I'm acutely aware now of the tender, shredded flesh of my face and the lack of pressure in my right eye. The frenzied throbbing in my brain intensifies with my anxiety. My head is about to cave in like a sledgehammered melon.

After all the hate I felt for her selfish actions, I think Sarah had the right idea. Her pain, her job woes, the bleakness of her world and the dismal relationships in it... like hers and mine... they're all gone now. No panic attacks. No fear. No struggle. No suffering.

She made it all stop forever. She always was the intelligent one…

As I battle to stay conscious, there remains only the ear-splitting sound of the massive ocean pounding out of sync with my tumultuous heartbeat and the hum of Sarah's voice.

I'm certain it's her.

Or maybe I've gone mad.

This horrifying arrhythmia is all that surrounds me now. The ocean's claustrophobic grip and the thumping of the swells are so familiar, as if I'm suffocating in a watery womb. Still, her voice gurgles on, singing sweetly.

I can see her now. Her arms are open, and crimson rivulets stream through the ebbing water from the gashes up her arm. They look like vibrant ribbons of seaweed growing from the crevices in her drained, pale skin. Her eyes are red and irritated, just like when I found her in the tub. She'd been crying, and I hadn't been there for her.

Now I'd be crying if I could. If I weren't encased in water already…

She smiles and drifts to me in the darkening, watery depths. The distance to the surface feels impossible now. I catch a fleeting glimpse of the racing sunset painted on the Atlantic's surface, rippling far above me as I'm dragged forcefully downward by the never-ending waves. Rusty glides carelessly overhead, eclipsing the tiny window of light shackled to me like an iron ball and chain.

Sarah opens her mouth. I can hear her words as plain as day through the saltwater. Her honeyed lips feel like home as they mouth the words I heard her say so often before that awful day. Before the memory of her in that tub became etched into my brain.

"Take a breath."

She smiles. It settles me.

"Take a breath," her angelic voice wisps through the seaweed and brine again, bringing me a singular moment of surprising comfort.

She looks different now. There are more teeth in her mouth than humanly possible. Sharpened, terrifying. The fear swells in my pulsating skull, mocking the power of the ocean as consciousness slips away.

"Take a breath," she murmurs one final time…

And I do.

TWO LIP GARDEN

An amber leaf abandoned the bough, danced joyfully down through the crisp night air, flitted like a moon-bathed butterfly through the darkness, and rested atop Lana Wilson's graying curls. Sheltered from the rest of the world behind a tall wall of trimmed privet bushes, a white beam sliced through the veil of darkness, illuminating brilliant pops of color throughout the yard. Another leaf followed, slipping through the humid air and twirling around a swarm of minuscule insects congregating wildly around the bulb of a work light on a strikingly vivid yellow stand.

She jammed the hand shovel into the rich, coffee-black soil and dug a hole a few inches deep. She placed a garlic-shaped tulip bulb, nestled in its protective organic sheath like the dry outer ring of an onion, pointy side up. She smiled.

Lana preferred to do her gardening at night. Darkness should never be feared, she thought. Since Gary's departure, tending to the earth seemed to pass the many long, sleepless hours between dusk and dawn. It allowed her to avoid the brutally searing afternoon sun, wicked New England winds, cold afternoon rains, and the chaotic noise of the blossoming suburban neighborhood, whose median age grew younger by the day.

She remembered the night of Gary's funeral, a gopher - or was it a squirrel? - laid waste to her veggie garden, shredding a cavity in the earth with its sharpened claws and running amok like some furry menace, gorging itself on a massive bed of romaine and cucumbers. Entranced by suffocating grief, she remembered kneeling down over the hole - or were they holes, plural? That evening, as darkness descended over the quiet Connecticut neighborhood like a sheet on a birdcage, Lana found herself filling in yet another dirt pit. Though the one Gary had been laid to rest in was deep and wide, this one seemed narrow and traveled fathoms downward into the unknown, piquing her curiosity. She wondered what the varmint was doing down there and if the gopher had a family of its own.

Something Lana knew she'd never have.

Lana stared blankly into the tiny, winding cavern with eyes shrouded by the thick plastic of her bifocals. As she pressed dirt down into the never-ending, hungry hole, she wondered if the critter had eaten the fruits of her labor by himself or if he had taken some back to its offspring.

She recalled a story her aunt up in Massachusetts had told her as a child about a blind mole who dug tunnels and deposited acorns in the dirt. The nuts turned into baby moles who would play among a burrowed system of offshoots until they had carved out a maze-like city underground with their claws, where they all lived happily ever after.

Happily ever after.

Pfft.

That term was the sure sign of a fairy tale, Lana thought. There weren't really 'happily ever afters' here on earth. Only pain, grief, and loneliness. There's misery and bad knees and creaky joints and crushing debt and mindless shopping and memory problems. There are rotting teeth and devastating car accidents. Sky-high property taxes. Inflation and anger. Rage and prescription medicines and abandonment and co-pays and insomnia and unpronounceable chemicals in food and hearts halting forever midway through a whiskey sour.

Reality is your husband keeling over on the dining room floor. The shattered glass once in his hand lying in a million pieces like your dreams of a life together. Dreams of a family. The twisted howl on his lips and the nightmarish bulge of his eyes... those were real.

Not acorns in the ground. Not a family of moles or gophers.

But fear... dying alone... loneliness.

Isolation.

Those are the real 'ever afters.'

Lana imagined how wonderful life would be if she had an acorn family. She wanted to plant a nut in the mud and spawn fresh human growth. To create a being she could nurture. One that could love her unconditionally.

A child who would never leave her like Gary did.

She imagined more of them, too, in the dirt, playing among the underground city like the foraging critters that had repeatedly decimated her crops.

But that was pure fantasy. Here she was, five years later — or was it six? — planting tulips at 3 a.m.

Lana scooped up two palms full of soil, mesmerized by the liver-spotted, once-taut skin on the back of her hands. She gingerly poured the dirt into the hole, over the bulb, and patted down. She couldn't wait to see the flower that would stem from it blossom brightly in the early spring after the final snow. Excited for the brilliant orange — or were they yellow? Salmon, perhaps? — buds she'd picked out in the store on her lunch break. Lana had fallen in love with the color, though she didn't recall what hue she'd chosen now, so the wait would only be that much more exciting when they revealed themselves. She only hoped she hadn't sowed it too close to another bulb. She couldn't remember if she'd already implanted some in this bed.

With another stab of the trowel, she spooned out a gob of powdery dirt and jabbed the implement back in again.

Click!

As the small spade made contact with something hard, she cocked her head curiously.

"Darned rocks." Her hot, visible breath oozed through the darkness as she muttered.

Click! Click-click!

As she prodded the soil with the silver point, it met repeatedly with the unyielding force beneath. She scraped the earth away from the object just beneath the loamy surface. The hard ivory exterior gleamed in the beam of the work light, and she examined it with ferocious interest.

"What in God's name?" Lana paddled frothy turf toward her, digging at the buried object like a terrier with both bare hands. A smooth surface with curves and ridges, whatever it was, seemed to extend much further throughout the bed. She dug faster, terrified at the sudden discovery. Lana gasped and pulled back, clutching two balled dirt-smudged hands to her face in horror.

Teeth.

Whatever it was... had teeth.

She realized quickly that she hadn't discovered a hunk of white rock, but instead, a glimmering human skull locked with its jaw in a forever scream buried in her garden. Lana imagined it must have been there a while because its lips and skin had long dissolved, and plant roots had wound around, choking the cavity with its tiny fingers where a left eye once sat.

Lana didn't know the next logical step. Should she call the police? Would they believe her? She'd probably sound like some mad woman calling the cops at this hour to explain the act of gardening, like a kook, while the rest of the world slumbered, ranting nonsense about flesh-devoid corpses in her tulip bed. And then there was the Alzheimers. It seemed from the outpouring of sympathy last year — or was it the one before? — that half the town had heard the tragic news about Lana's dementia by now.

Perhaps...

This all can wait until morning, she thought.

Maybe then, the police would see her instead as an early bird, tending to her flower garden at dawn with a morning cup of coffee, like a sane person, and they'd be more likely to take her seriously.

She gathered the courage to examine the skull, wiping the dirt from its brow. The head looked small, like a child.

Who would do something so atrocious?

Was this all just a prank at her expense? Or did someone think an elderly woman's yard would be a perfect place to hide a cadaver?

Lana looked down at the screaming skinless face of the fledgling before her and wished she'd have had children of her own. She longed for something small and meek in need of nurturing and care.

Always did.

That's why she went so ballistic in the final months of Gary's life. Not only had her husband been rumored to have participated in and even instigated several torrid affairs, but he even had allegedly fathered some children in Hamden somewhere.

The latter hurt Lana far more than the former.

She wanted nothing more than to be a mother. Nothing more than to hold a child in her hands for comfort, giving it tenderness and adoration, just the way she displayed love for so many other things in life. She had a way of making the world richer and more beguiling one dahlia bulb, varnished deck board, trimmed privet, or painted wall at a time. Lana was a creator, hell-bent on leaving the earth more lovely than it had been loaned to her. She battled the destructive forces of the universe daily with every ounce of effort within her. With more on this planet like her, the world would surely be a better place, she thought.

Lana always wanted to impart those values and virtues to her own little one.

Or two.

She chuckled at the heartbreaking irony. Despite her ability to up-cycle, build, and beautify things around her, she wasn't capable of the most important yet simplest creation of all. The one womankind was biologically made for.

When she and Gary married in her twenties, they tried to have their own 'brood.' (Gary's words, not hers.) Back then, he claimed to have similar goals in life, wanting a son to play baseball in this very backyard. He'd selected hypothetical names for a girl and threatened her future non-existent boyfriends that if they ever wronged her, they'd feel the cold shock of Gary's wrath and, quite possibly, his 9 mm pistol as well.

After years of trying to keep up with her husband's voracious sexual appetite and newfound deviances, she begged Gary to adopt shortly after the rumors started. He'd shut her down with ever-changing reasons:

It wasn't the right time financially. He wasn't sure he wanted to bring a child into this 'crazy world.' Kids were too expensive. Without them, they'd still have time and freedom to travel.

But they hadn't traveled much by then, and, in retrospect, they never would. Beyond the trips to Fairhope to see Gary's siblings, they hadn't ventured further than New England since the honeymoon.

By then, her age was a factor. She was only in her mid-forties at the time. A dangerous time period to be having a baby, admittedly. But she hadn't yet hit menopause and was willing to accept those risks. She was ready to sacrifice her life if need be to carry forth a small piece of herself to continue her legacy. And should her offspring have special needs, she was prepared for that commitment, too. She wanted someone to love and hold, to witness them grow and blossom like her garden, no matter its IQ or abilities.

Gary wouldn't even entertain it.

Now here she was, hovering over someone else's child, encased in dark earth like someone's buried family dog. A fragmented human being born from two wholes, still and lifeless, plastered into an eternal, horrified scream. Or laugh. A hearty chuckle, perhaps, at how cruel and unfair the world is.

Lana could relate.

She wanted to pick the cadaver and hold it, to cradle its sterling skeleton in her arms and remind them that they are in a better place now, cooing with a loving tone, just as a caring mother would. She wanted to wipe the dirt from his face like rich chocolate cake from a boy's cheek.

...Until the police showed up in their khaki uniforms, trampling her flowerbed without consequence, excavating body parts as if her beloved garden didn't exist.

Maybe until then, he could be hers.

She would keep him company, sweeping worms from the cavity where his fleshy tongue used to be. The bond they shared in the wee hours of the morning could be theirs to share for eternity. And she'd know, even briefly, what it was like to be a mother. To adore and protect something so fragile.

The morbidity made her think, too, about Gary. About the similar expression he made when he died and the stillness she sensed throughout the room. She felt his life escape through the air and the ether, leaving her feeling oddly less forsaken and alone than she'd been moments before when he'd been standing right in front of her, breathing just fine. Sometimes, being together was more lonely than her widowed years to follow. At least then, she had support from friends, relatives, and neighbors.

Tears welled in Lana's eyes, dripping on the skeletal remains of the childlike, hot, drizzling rain. On nights like tonight, when she had moments of clarity through the snapping jaws of dementia as it gnawed a lifetime full of treasured memories away for good, she was grateful for the privacy provided by gardening at night. She often cried — she remembered now — spilling warm tears into the garden bed whenever she thought of Gary.

Or of Gary's children...

She'd met them once at the funeral. She saw them both. A boy and a girl, young and fresh-faced. Their dark brown eyes were locked on the grayed corpse in Gary's silvery opalescent casket - or was it black? A woman, the mother, held the hand of the girl. They wept solemnly, and Lana eyed them intently. They were the only people at the viewing that she didn't recognize. That, she recollected with lucidity.

The foreignness of their faces was burned into her splintering brain. She introduced herself as Lana Wilson, Gary's wife, and she remembered the panic on the woman's face and the expressions of confusion flashing across the children's precious eyes. The boy looked like Gary's childhood photos.

Spitting image, some might say.

It occurred to her that that had been the reason Gary had flip-flopped on wanting children. He already enjoyed the miraculous joy of creating life with someone else...

Twice.

Lana collapsed, she recalled. Thumped forcefully to her degrading knees and frail wrists, more embarrassed than injured. The mistress offered to help her up, but Lana swatted her away like a demon, blubbering violently, incoherent.

The brunette stranger was gorgeous and curvaceous, with full-pouting lips and youthful glowing skin. She had to be at least a decade and a half younger than Lana. To her devastation, the rumors proved true.

How was someone capable of such a thing? How could one possibly live a double life so nonchalantly? Hurting those around him with carefree abandon.

In any fair world, those two adorable kids should've been hers. They should have been throwing curve balls over the dirt where Lana knelt on the foam pad above the skeletal remains. Two kids with stark resemblances to his espresso-colored eyes and mouths full of his exceptional teeth. They'd have her hair and Gary's hearty head-back belly laugh. His wide-mouthed, genuine cackle was like the one that the adolescent's skull was frozen in.

If Gary hadn't died, she'd have killed him herself, she thought. She meant it, too. Watching him suffer the massive heart attack seemed tragic at the time but nowhere near as horrendous as the face he'd have made if Lana had learned, while he was still alive and kicking, about the secret double-life.

Rage bubbled up inside Lana like a wicked vat of acid dripping poisonous tendrils around her heart and throat and clamping down tightly in a choke-hold like tightening wisteria vines. She dropped the trowel into the dirt and strained to get up with an audible hip pop and patellas crunching beneath the weight of her aging body. She shuffled across the manicured Kentucky bluegrass and pulled open the screen door in search of a glass of cold water to help her get a grip on things. She felt her blood pressure pound hard in her head at the fury still brewing toward Gary.

Her head pounded, throbbing loudly in her skull just as it had years ago when she'd cleaned out Gary's old metal file cabinet and found proof of his vasectomy. This had been news to Lana. And it explained a lot. For years, she'd woefully blamed herself for being infertile when it had been him and another colossal decades-long lie he left behind for her to find like some twisted scavenger hunt. The receipts had been as devastating as his death.

Perhaps more so.

Once inside, she flicked on the kitchen light, and her thunderous heart pounded up into her throat again.

Slumped in a heap on the floor, a young girl sat, still in a puddle of blood. Lana wanted to scream but trembled instead. Her dirt-covered slipper touched the end of the sanguine pool, drying to a dark, horrific shade of rusty brown.

She stepped toward the girl cautiously, worried that she might awaken and scare Lana to death. But the girl sagged, lifeless, and rumpled. The room felt as truly empty as it had been when Gary passed. Lana pulled her soil-encrusted hands to her face and realized that her elbows and upper arms were covered in dried blood. Reddish streaks mixed with dark dirt engulfed her. She looked down.

Her entire nightgown was caked in blood.

Had she done this?

Was she capable?

Tears fell again from her wrinkled eyes at the frustration of the dementia haze settling in like a fog on her brain. She approached the dead girl, clad in drenched jeans and a t-shirt, her dirty dishwater blond hair pulled back in a ponytail. It was the same dull shade of blond as Gary's hair. With a crooked, arthritic finger, she tipped the girl's head upward to examine it, and her eyes widened. Though she'd only seen them once — or was it twice? Or maybe…

Lana knew those hooded brown eyes anywhere. It was the girl from the funeral.

Gary's daughter.

With Gary's eyes.

The resemblance was even stronger than the last time she'd seen the girl.

But how? Why?

Suddenly, Lana's mind remembered. Flashes. Troubling bits of things. Like a mind flipping through radio stations rapidly, never getting a full song. She recalled bits of recent memories from earlier in the night. She recalled opening the door for the girl, inviting her in. She seemed timid, uneasy, and confused. A couch. An embrace. Lana went to fetch a cake from the fridge. The girl inquired about her brother's whereabouts. She recollected her saying something about him having been missing for some time. Years... possibly.

Lana insisted the girl enjoy a sliver of chocolate cake. Protests. The girl started toward the door just before Lana drove the knife she'd used to slice the dessert right into the girl's throat.

Everything went foggy for a bit, but she remembered the teen's voice screaming, "Why, why, why?" as she bumbled through the house.

Lana peered into the darkened living room, dimly lit by the bloom of an ancient, dusty kitchen fixture near the doorway. She saw smears and splotches of drying blood all over the room. Dried hand prints on the walls. The girl had put up a fight.

But she was home now.

Yes, Lana remembered. She's come home so that we can be a family at last.

***

Lana lay on her side across the churned soil of the tulip garden. It was a flower-adorned grave site masked from the world by tightly trimmed privet bushes and the cloak of the darkened night sky. She affectionately caressed the cold, pale cheek of the young girl in awe of her childlike beauty and forever-locked youth.

It had been an exhausting task for a woman of Lana's age to drag that much limp dead weight all the way out there to the garden...

But now it was a family reunion as she was laid to rest near her brother.

This, Lana remembered more lucidly than anything in her recent years, had been the goal all along. To be reunited with her children. To rejoin her with two treasured beings to nurture each night in the garden and watch them grow like the tulips planted above them.

They would be a surprise, no, a gift, to herself that, with such a fractured mind, she could receive many times over through the coming years just as though every time was the first time.

She would tuck her beloved children into the earth, snuggling them intimately for a long

207

slumber with covers made of soil and roots. With a simple trowel full of dirt, she could hold their hands and keep them from being scared of the dark, as darkness was nothing to fear. She'd sing them to sleep every night here in the garden. Their tears of joy from having such a loving, doting mother would water the flowers above them, keeping prying eyes at bay.

No one would tear them apart. She caressed the boy's skull and planted a goodnight kiss on the girl's lips before tucking them in beneath the soil, among the bulbs that would burst forth new growth and beauty in the earliest of spring once the frost had passed.

She patted down the last of the dirt and stared up at the early morning sunrise, at last, exhausted enough for her weary, confused mind to sleep.

***

As she lay in bed, listening to the playful morning birds chirp ecstatic tunes, she thought about her children and how exciting it would be to watch them grow through the future marked by a breathtaking display of bold and vibrant colored flowers on thick green foliage and long straw-like stems blooming in every color of the rainbow.

She couldn't wait to unearth them both and find them beneath the soil again next year. Most likely by accident, due to dementia, turning momentary horror into joy all over again once she pieced the past together. It would be a true surprise and absolute delight for her fractured mind to rediscover, just as she'd rediscovered the boy every year for the several before.

And now, they were all a family at last.

In the months until their next reunion, she would love and tend to the garden with her stiff back and trembling bony fingers covered in ultra-soft skin as if she were the goddess Mother Nature herself.

If only Gary could see her now... reveling in her true happily ever after with her complete and loving acorn family...

Finally, a mother, after all.

FEED THE MACHINE

Stuart pinched a cigarette between thin lips and sucked back the last shreds of thick tobacco it had to offer. His bony hand trembled as he flung the spent butt into a bed of crimson petunias against the brick building. His face was milk white, making the reddened rings around his eyes stand out. Despite the nausea, his callous wit was still present. "Rollin' 'ose pants up makes you look like the fuckin' chimney sweep in Mary Poppins." His thick London accent laced every word as he playfully indicated Dash's calves with a sharp nod.

"Please, mate. Not now." Dash's cadence and pronunciation were similar to Stuart's, but the words, thick with guilt, fell cold from his colorless lips. He squatted on the steps and sucked slow drags of air to soothe waves of

211

sickness pulsing through him. He glared at the biohazard dumpster tucked against the building, imagining the soup of sun-marinating ichor and shredded tissue dwelling within. It was a simmering kettle of once-bloodshot eyes and frail, carpal tunnel-ridden arms. His face, damp with sweat, grew colorless as he wretched loudly over the side rail, tasting his morning snack of brie and crackers for the second time.

"How a' you not frowin' up too? Fuckin' sociopath."

Dash stared in horror. Stuart remained unfazed by the traumatic events of the morning. He was not without sympathy. He'd simply had months more experience with the blood and gore that had been shed.

Dash's childhood friend had always gotten him into seedy situations, but this…

This took the cake.

Stuart shrugged. "Eh, gets easier, bruv."

Dash glared up with two hazel orbs infused with disgust. Of all of the sleazy schemes for a quick buck Stuart had involved him in over the years, his friend always had a way of normalizing the trauma and making everything seem like just an average day. Nothing ever seemed to rattle Stuart Campbell.

"It's like 'ey say, video games desensitize." Stuart managed a smile, flashing a dingy row of abused English teeth. "Seems fucked now, bruv, but trust. Friday when we get paychecks, you'll wanna kiss 'is geeza's feet." He thumbed himself proudly in the chest. "Couple months 'a this an' we go back to Mayfair, go find 'at West End bird who mugged you off at Berkeley Square."

Dash dabbed his bile-covered lips with the back of his hand. "Saundra."

"Saundra! 'At's it." Stuart laughed, exhaling smoke out in rapid puffs like a chugging locomotive. "By June you' be able 'a flaunt enough quid ta' buy 'at daft slag's flat outright, if you wanted to."

Dash managed to stand, weakly dusting off the knees of his rolled pants.

"That'll be the life. You an' me, downin' top-shelf bevvys til' we're absolutely pissed, 'avin' good laugh, watchin' all them birds graft for Paul-William Pritchett's attention. You'll 'ave your pick of any. Money's the ultimate equalizer, bruv. You'll see."

"You know I hate it when you fuckin' call me that."

"Yeah, but it got you on ya' feet, innit? You twat."

Stuart motioned to the door, and Dash shook his head. It was time to face the gruesome scene inside.

***

The room was wall-to-wall gore, worse than any crime scene photo Dash had ever stumbled upon, even as a morbid teen questing for the most vile sites the internet had to offer. The Faces of Death VHS he'd stolen from his father's bureau as a teenager couldn't compare to this.

This was real. In the flesh.

Death, up close and personal.

He felt sickness wash back over him and feared his own vomit would only intensify the already intense cleanup and sterilization regimen. This morning, the walls were arctic white, reflective as a mirror. Now, those same walls were caked in copious amounts of rust-colored arterial spray, like a cursive love letter written in ruby ink, punctuated with knotted hunks of tissue and a shredded organ post-script in the puddle on the floor.

He wondered how life's path had led him to this morally perverted moment where the disregard for human life in the quest for personal home entertainment had become so normalized.

Stuart, now clad in a stark white, disposable, protective painter's uniform and gray ventilation mask, rolled a canary-yellow bucket into the gore-spattered testing room by the stained mop, sloshing amid a pungent industrial-strength cleaning solution. The wafting stench of bleach and lavender seeped through the mask, overpowering the room's coppery penny scent.

Muffled by the filter, Stuart's accent drifted through the stillness. "It's like being inside the microwave after some bloke's jus' nuked a kitten on high for ten minutes."

Dash didn't laugh. He imagined humor helped Stuart cope with the gore, and allowed him to detach from the weighty guilt and moral ramifications of the job. He peered down at a lonesome hunk of a human skull with a bit of scalp and full eyebrow still attached, along with the detached remnants of ocular musculature. He scooped it up in a gloved hand, accidentally smearing viscous brain matter across the fingers of his yellow rubber gloves. Disgusted, he slid it into a plastic rubbish bag and winced at the wet thunk it made as it smacked against the tile beneath.

"'Member mum's second husband?" Stuart asked out of nowhere, mopping up a lake of dark brown blood.

"Johnny?" Dash breathed slow and deep through his mask and attempted to calm himself before the onset of anxious hyperventilation. "Right swell geeza', he was."

"Remember when we lived at that flat on Wardour Street and John had that little room upstairs wiv' all the arcade games?"

Dash nodded, numbly locating the remainder of the cratered, dismembered head of the deceased. Clawed apart, the male subject's youthful flesh was ripped into the fragmented pieces of a gory puzzle, impossible to reassemble.

"Remember that one summer, we were up there for the better part'a two weeks playing that Queen's Quest game where you had to jump through that castle dungeon and collect all 'em gemstones?" Stuart chuckled.

Dash remembered, alright. Suddenly, he could breathe again, immersing himself in childhood memories to escape the surrounding horrors.

Stuart regaled. "'Member, at one point, Johnny caught us? He was so mad, but when he found out how many pounds we'd put in that thing, he changed his tune!" Stuart's mask-muffled giggle rang out through the room. It reminded Dash of Stuart as a younger boy, jovial at even the darkest times. "'At geeza'd made a fortune off us!"

"Remember what he hollered at us the next day?" Dash yelled. "Best get upstairs…"

Chuckling, both howled into the air in unison:

"It's time ta' feed the machine!"

Dash emitted a belly laugh and approached the subject slab, the obvious epicenter of the pints of spilled blood and gruesome, fleshy carnage. With a gloved hand, he tugged a hunk of human trapezius from the leather neck restraint, the musculature still attached to a gleaming, exposed collarbone, and dropped it in his trash bag with a thwack.

He watched his best friend work diligently, chipping away at the lumps of stomach-turning ichor as if picking up roadside trash for community service. All he needed was a blinding neon vest and a spiked gig to complete the look.

Concentrating hard, Stuart coiled a graying pile of soft lower intestines into his sack as if wrangling a muddy garden hose. The subject's muddy bowel contents oozed through the claw marks in the shredded tissue. Leaking like a sieve, the revolting gore slopped against the thin plastic of the bag. No longer even wincing, the repugnant stench permeating into his suit was something he had strangely come to terms with.

Dash had long ago taken anatomy and physiology at uni, but the mangled state of scattered organs, splintered bones, and frayed musculature made identification of the mutilated mess difficult. He found a wet hunk of something, shredded like slippery pulled pork, only darker, and slid it gingerly into the black plastic. He wondered what it was.

A liver, perhaps? Kidney?

Dash escaped back into the nostalgia of days long gone in John's forbidden home arcade. The dust. The cluttered, cramped space where two kids could squeeze in and forget about life for a few hours. The dilapidated wooden housings. The graveyard of broken screens and chipped joysticks...

It was bliss.

He recalled how the dank room effused potent wafts of cedar mixed with hot, ancient plastic. He could still hear the delirious repetition of the Queen's Cave theme song as it beeped on a melodic loop like bizarre techno music. He tune. Quiet, muffled notes wafted from his mask.

As soon as Stuart heard the tune, he joined in, crescendoing until their muffled voices bounced off of every gruesome surface of what remained of the carcass of subject #482.

***

"Relax. The topical takes a moment to sink in," Dr. Angus said, the tone of her voice caring as she patted the young man's arm. Her thick Tennessee accent was unmistakable despite her attempt to mask it, and the honeyed color of her silken hair glimmered beneath the luminous fluorescent overhead lights.

"Sorry, I'm just stoked." Anthony's voice wavered, his throat wriggling anxiously against the neck restraint. "This is fucking awesome." He grinned with a mouthful of plaque-ridden teeth the shade of a crusty ring on a convenience store toilet.

"It really is. I'm glad you see that. Not everyone appreciates it the way you do. You're part of ground-breaking work, Anthony. Thanks to you, when Verity launches worldwide, this technology will make the P.S. and P.C. virtual reality machines of the past look like the Atari by comparison." Her pearl-white smile disarmed him.

"Jesus, I forgot Atari was even a thing."

"I'm sure it was before your time."

219

"Yep." He grinned. His smirk was smug, cocky. "But, if anyone should be a part of this, it's me."

In the privacy of the observation booth, Dash rolled his eyes.

Stuart laughed aloud, kicking his feet onto the control panel. "Fuckin' wanker, 'is one is."

Back in the room, the smug American prattled on.

"Seriously, you don't want some scrub rating the quality of your system. You want a discerning gamer like moi." He tried to press his hand to his chest, forgetting it was bound to the sterilized patient lounger by a leather strap, sending a jiggling shock wave through the rest of his doughy chest. Though appearing slender overall, the young man was soft, with little muscle definition beyond his yammering jaw and two strapped, sinewy forearms.

"My Twitch channel's hella successful. I'm no idiot. Million-and-a-half followers there. Another half-mil on Tiktok. Discord's blowin' up. Sponsors out the bung-hole begging for some word-'a-mouth exposure and some fuckin' ad space on my sites. So this could be pretty big for y'all… if this thing don't suck."

Dr. Angus clenched her jaw subconsciously, pretending to listen as she finished connecting the wires and receptor units. "I assure you, you've never experienced anything like this system before."

"Cool. 'Cuz I don't push games and systems I don't believe in. Y'know, people in the community value what I have to say. So," he tried to shrug but only shook the table, "blow my mind, and this could be huge for you. Give me perfect optimization or... something over 150 frames per second. Or a storyline that's fresh as hell. Or, ya know, lemme see something I'd need a graphics card built by NASA for, and then I'll sing your praises all over the internet."

A dark mess of unkempt hair framed his angular face, unbrushed like a youthful, crazed scientist. One of the attached wires dragged a lock of it across his face. He tried to raise a thin, bony wrist but remembered he was locked to the slab by restraints around his elbows.

"Can you scratch my face for me?" Anthony winced and wriggled his nose, tickled by the scraggly strays.

She obliged. He couldn't have been more than twenty-three, but he had an air of self-congratulatory immaturity like that of a stunted teenager.

"I'm glad I get to be first." He beamed.

"Oh," she chuckled coyly. "Lord, no. You're hardly the first."

"Hmm. That so?" His demeanor was crestfallen.

"You're actually subject," Dr. Angus looked at her metal clipboard, "number 483." A grin crept across her attractive face, silently celebrating that this encounter was more than likely the last time she'd ever have to deal with the insufferable incel.

At least… alive.

"Stuart, is all of 483's paperwork in order?" Dr. Angus peered up at the booth, gorgeous in spite of her thick-framed glasses.

Stuart leaned into the microphone and spoke. The Brit's voice boomed through loudspeakers overhead.

"Affirmative. Contracts were all digitally signed half an hour ago. Dash filed all the health, hazard, and liability waivers wiv' legal. We've got the green light. Good to go." Through the window, he gave a bony thumbs up and kicked back again.

"Yeah, I peeped the contracts. They all looked fairly standard," Anthony said confidently.

In the observation booth, Stuart burst into laughter. "This fuck is right stupid, he is."

Dr. Angus rolled her chair behind the slab and pulled a sterile probe from the small tray beside Anthony's head. "Number 483, do you feel this?" She pressed her thumb up into the base of his skull through a gap in the headrest.

His black, beady, ferret-like eyes locked with Stuart's through the window as he shook his head. "Nah."

Dr. Angus activated a lever. The hydraulic slab raised like a car on a mechanic's lift. She slid her rolling chair beneath him, palpated his vertebrae, and pressed the needle end of the probe deep into the tender flesh of his neck. "You might feel a slight pinch."

"Jesus CHRIST!" Anthony wailed in pain and heaved against the restraints. His words were drawn out in his southern accent, whiny.

"Alright. You're doing great, 483." Angus lowered the chair and rifled through the contents of the tray. She squeezed a metal clamp, and its hardened jaws opened wide. She latched it down over his face.

Anthony began to pant, claustrophobia creeping in on him. "Wait, what?"

"Next, we must insert both ocular probes." She pulled a needled pair of cables that hung from the cords connected to his spine.

"Awww, hell no!" Anthony's breath reeked foulness upward into her face as he hollered. He thrust his arms against the restraints. His legs quaked, bound tightly by both ankles. Panic steeped into his racing heart. Reality set in.

He had no recourse.

He could do nothing.

"Don't worry. This process was fully explained in the paperwork." With care, she clamped another contraption on one of his eyelids and pinched the eye closed. He cried out.

"Stop! Bitch, that form was like… 26 pages long! How was I supposed to read it all?"

"Like you said, 483. You're no idiot. There was no time limit."

"No one reads that shit!" Anthony jerked his lid as she clamped his other eye.

The reverberations of Anthony's screams vibrated the viewing booth. The shrill wails sent an empathetic shiver through Dash like a rush of icy slush through his veins. He longed for the moment when the screaming stopped.

The subject's voice, laden with childlike terror, bounced around the echoing, sterile chamber, and the muted cries seethed into the booth.

"I gotta get some fresh air. I still don't think I can handle this part yet." Dash's look was apologetic as he squeezed through the door and exited into the hallway. Stuart returned his eerily calm gaze back to the monitors.

Back at the subject slab, Dr. Angus had finally clamped Anthony's second eye shut. "Relax, 483. You opted for our most terrifying game. I'm afraid this is the easy part." She patted his shoulder in a phony attempt to comfort him. Secretly, she'd begun to feel nothing about this process. In fact, she thought, there were worse ways to make a buck.

Anthony grew quiet, paralyzed with fear. Bright overhead lights bleakly blurred through the blood vessels and veins in his eyelids, obscuring his vision to a murky amber glow.

"What... what are you doing now?" He fearfully uttered the words.

Without further explanation, Dr. Angus skillfully slid the sharp, hypodermic end of the first thin, metal probe through the fleshy corner of his left lid, careful not to puncture the eyeball itself and ruin the experience. She'd done that with Number 12 and beat herself up about it ever since, reminding herself constantly:

You were new. You were learning. Nobody's perfect.

Anthony shrieked like a braying donkey as the needle slid into his face, nestling against the bones of his skull. His cry was pure, chilling.

"Make a note, Stuart. Next time, we need a clamp for the lips, too." Angus chuckled and looked toward the window. But Stuart didn't laugh. She'd made the same joke several times before.

He thought about holding down the intercom and telling her to get some new material, but he opted against it. She was normally so straight-laced. He'd let her recycle her stale material. No harm in it, he thought.

Dr. Angus inserted the second probe stealthily, and Anthony screeched again. "Stuart, ocular probes, successful. Eyeballs need no re-inflation." She turned back to Anthony. "Alright, 483. Are you ready to start the game?"

Terrified silence from the pinned, penetrated patient. Tears squeezed out of the tugged slits near the probes, which made him feel like one of the splayed-open, dissected frogs he'd abused in high school biology.

"As you know, 483, this gaming system is called Verity. It is a unique fourth-dimensional reality system where your body becomes the console. The experience you've chosen, Bloodshed, developed in Japan, comes to you via sophisticated electric pulses and frequencies from probes inserted between your cervical vertebrae and medial rectus muscles of both eyes. Together they can relay information constantly to get your eyes, nervous system, and brain all in perfect tune for harmonious sensory programming."

Stuart typed a command into the software and flashed another thumbs up to Angus while the software booted. She acknowledged.

"By plugging directly into the body and brain, the system also uses these impulses to stimulate the olfactory system simulating smells of the game, as well as nerve receptors to simulate touch and pain. There are auditory hallucinations that coincide with the program as well. Better than surround sound, but they are not quite as sophisticated as the rest," she giggled. "It is still in the alpha testing phase, after all. So to bridge any gaps, we will be placing earmuffs on you which will play the soundtrack the designers created to coincide with the Bloodshed software."

"While insertion was unpleasant, our sister laboratory in Louisiana is working on implant technology involving surgically-installed ports that stay in the body after a brief procedure. That way, once installed, cables and new game cards with creator or user-created downloadable content can be inserted into the dorsal port like an iPod's auxiliary cord into a CD player."

"I know," she laughed, "I'm dating myself with the reference. People don't like corded devices anymore, so the Louisiana branch is already working on Bluetooth connectivity as well. But for now," Angus patted her knees, "you're here to alpha test Bloodshed, the first horror game ever designed for technology. It is intended to rival Hideo Kojima and Konami games like P.T. and such. But you already know all about those, I'm sure, being a cutting-edge elite gamer."

Anthony remained quiet, salty tears like little streams around his ocular probes.

Dr. Angus rose, clutching a corded portable computer unit. She selected an item from the screen. "This was an exceptional choice, by the way. Bloodshed isn't tested nearly as often as Vacationland. Many subjects prefer to opt for the family-friendly game, but this is the one that really needs the most testing and polish, in my opinion." Her chuckle had a sinister tinge to it, like a creamy drink with a garnish of sadism.

"You should see the home screen shortly," she concluded, typing a ten-digit code into the keypad.

Stuart pressed the button and spoke into the microphone. "Image's up. Subject 483 should be experiencing opening menu momentarily."

Anthony shivered, clammy, probes jutting from both eyes. They bobbed subtly with panicked eye movements. Below the metal eyelid pincers, his lips trembled, agape in awe and horror. However, his expression quickly shifted.

What he saw was like nothing he'd ever experienced before. Anthony was no longer on some stainless steel slab in Nashville, harnessed like a collared dog, plugged in like a Sega Genesis.

No.

He was visually transported somewhere else entirely. It felt like a lucid dream. He willed his mind to look at his body. His hands were no longer shackled but free to move in any direction. The colors of the menu screen were dazzling, like ominous technicolor. He imagined this would be how Tokyo looked at night, lit up with vibrant neons bursting through the darkness of a night sky. He was a replica of himself... an illusion at his current age, standing in a foreign, fantastic place.

"Holy shit." A smile crept through his day-old patchy stubble, and his grungy teeth beamed through a spreading smile. "This... this is awesome."

Dr Angus laughed at the patient's rapid emotional turnaround. It was common, but it still never failed to amuse her.

"Now, you only get one crack at the game," Angus said, hoping Anthony was paying attention.

In the booth, Stuart muttered to himself quietly. "Or rather, the game gets one crack at you."

Dr. Angus went through her paper checklist, which was clamped to a clipboard. "Now, through the building to your right, there's a clothing store. The game has this section unlocked currently, so you have access to whatever outfit you'd like. When the system is available worldwide, many of the outfits will only be available through in-game purchases or unlockable achievements."

Anthony wasn't listening to a word she said. Inside the ominous clothing store, he was already dressing in his chosen outfit: a pair of torn skinny jeans, a muscle tank, a tattered leather jacket, and stylish chucks. He modeled them in front of a full-length mirror and then proudly yelled, "Done!"

"Alright, now it's time for the brief training tutorial where we can test the functionality of all of the sensory nodes to make sure everything's working correctly. After that, you can start the game. Sound good?"

"Great. Let's get it on." Anthony was grinning fully now.

Angus nodded to Stuart and placed a large set of vintage-looking headphones around Anthony's ears, nudging them exactly into place. Stuart booted up the training software with the deft click of several keys.

With a dramatic whoosh, Anthony was transported to a California hilltop overlooking a raging forest fire. The overpowering scent of so much burning wood before him was noxious. He coughed. Smoke billowed from the torched throng of trees in the distance of the singed hellscape. Ash rained from the sky, clinging to his leather jacket and powdering his fresh kicks with soot.

He reached out a hand. In reality, the hand was strapped to the table, twitching in his restraints, but in the new world, it moved freely. He rubbed the falling flakes of ash on his fingers. They smeared across the tips and stuck to them.

"Wow. This is really something." Anthony's voice was louder than he intended due to the earmuffs. His mouth was slack, hung open in concentration and wonderment, no longer concerned with the needles or restraints.

He could hear the crackle of the fire, too, all around him, in perfect surround sound. It roared and crackled. Behind it wafted ethereal human screams. Screams of relentless pain emanated from beyond the fiery treeline.

"Holy shit." His tone was quiet, reverential.

"Shit, bruv," Stuart mumbled to himself. "Shoulda held out for the x-rated program they're working on."

"Un... fucking... believable!" Anthony's head turned slightly, tugging taut the cords of the eye probes.

Dr. Angus touched Anthony's fingertips and transferred ash from his strapped hand to hers. Satisfied, she held up her finger so Stuart could see the transmittal in the booth. He notated the finding in his report with the rapid clicks of his keys.

"Walk around, 483. Get used to the mental controls. Verity wants to give you the best fighting chance possible." Dr. Angus stared at the handheld monitor, viewing what Anthony was seeing and scanning the scrolling code overlay for the sounds and scents currently experienced.

Dash slunk into the observation room, pale and quiet. "What'd I miss?"

"Aye, the lad popped a chub for the clothing store. He's in the forest fire training now. Angus touched his hand. He's got the ash transfer. All systems are go."

"Eva' wonda' how any of this works?"

"Mate, 'at's above my pay grade, innit?" Stuart snorted, and both men returned their gazes to the garbled real-time image streaming on the screen. On a neighboring monitor, gobs of code whirled up a tar-black screen.

"Over, under… ten minutes. How long'll he last?"

"Under. Way under for this cocky prick. Hell, I got an extra tenner on him givin' up the ghost under five. 'Is bloke won't make it past Toothy." Dash folded his bony arms.

"Oof. Really? Figured he'd get to Axe Man, at least. But, yeh, he is a bit on the wimpy side." Stuart slapped the desk. "Shit, you know what, I'll take that action."

Angus's voice bled through the partition. "Tutorial complete, fellas. 483 is ready to start the game."

"Copy." Dash spoke into the intercom.

Stuart inputted some commands and pressed both the intercom and patient audio override buttons simultaneously. "All set. Welcome to Bloodbaf', mate."

He released the buttons and leaned so far back in his seat that Dash thought he might topple. "Time to feed the machine, innit?"

Dash snickered. "Cleva', mate."

Anthony's hands twitched bizarrely as he fumbled through dark nothingness.

"I can't see anything!" Anthony panicked, fearing the game had malfunctioned.

Dash pressed the audio override button. "You're in a room, mate. You 'ave to find an exit." He released the button and shook his head as if it should have been common knowledge. "See, Stu, shoulda taken the under."

"Oh, gotcha." Anthony's response was quiet. His hands caressed the rough, cold concrete walls of the pitch-black room in search of an exit. "Jesus, this feels so real. Unbelievable."

Dr. Angus watched the depressions on the patient's fingertips as they pressed into the flat surface of the walls. She dropped her eyes to the monitor as Anthony found the knob and released himself into the darkened, blood-spattered halls of a middle school. The hallway offered mirrored rows of glinting lockers but little light. One dying, overhead fluorescent tube flickered repeatedly, setting a sinister tone, dying and then reviving with a chilling buzz. The electrical hum grew louder as he neared the source.

BAM!

The sound of piled wooden chairs smashing to the ground rang out beside him.

"Jesus!" Anthony hollered out, alarmed by the jarring activity so close to him, exciting every sense.

In the school, a thunderous crash of wood and metal swept through the reverberating halls. Something slowly crept nearby. Every wet, nasty step of the thing sent a chill through him.

His heart thumped against his strapped chest.

In the game, terror stopped him cold. His character was frozen in place, feet glued to the ground as he listened to that... thing... whatever it was, rustle nearby.

He scanned his surroundings. Moonlight seeped through the blinds, bathing his soot-covered attire. He entered, choosing to investigate the noise. As he inched inward, he dragged his hands over the wood of the overturned desks. Hot, viscous liquid coated them. His chucks slipped on a broad, wine-colored puddle on the floor. He hunched down, examining the coagulating blood closer. A waft of copper filled his nostrils.

"Ewwww, cool," Anthony murmured.

Dr. Angus saw the tacky, garnet smears appear on his palms, some transferring to the armrests beneath him.

483 times.

483 times she had done this, and still it never ceased to astound her how the real and virtual worlds could be so interconnected. How these manufactured happenings could manifest on her plane of existence….

In her reality.

She couldn't fathom the years of development Sakamant Talagashi's team put into the sophisticated probe tech over the last few decades to make true virtual reality possible.

Anthony peered into a shattered, blood-soaked aquarium at the horrific remains of a furry class pet, its innards tangled, wound in its metal exercise wheel behind four jagged walls of busted glass. He crinkled his nose in disgust.

The class clock chimed overhead as he examined the sinister school bloodbath. He wondered what had transpired, allowing his mind to wander to sick and devious places.

Chilling sounds infiltrated. Suspenseful instrumental music arose with clarity from seemingly nowhere, like an invisible string quartet inhabited the room with him. The orchestra swelled.

A shadow.

In the hallway.

It was impossibly large, shrinking with every nearing step…

Something was coming.

Anthony tensed. He watched the darkness shift across checkered laminate squares. He listened. Wet, ear-splitting slapping. Deep, phlegm-ridden breathing. Thumping feet pounding. He could feel it, too. Colossal vibrations of nearing, massive feet pulsated through him, spreading all the way to his bones.

And more than anything, he could smell it. Smell the vile odor of bloated roadkill. Smell the rancid wafts of excrement and pungent piss. He wanted to vomit.

As the unseen beast closed in, Anthony hopped on a ledge near the windows, smashed a pile of nondescript science books onto the floor with his bloody, ash-stained shoes, and yanked open a window. His attempt to flee was thwarted immediately. He was at least 10 stories in the night air with nothing to catch his fall. Jumping wasn't an option.

"I'd recommend a weapon, 483," Stuart said, poking the audio override.

Dash objected, mocking a ref's whistle-blow and tossing his arms in the air. "Oi, dirty play, bruv. Free kick! Come on!"

"I'm sorry!" Stuart jokingly apologized. "The lad's an idiot! I had to!"

"Cheatin' twat!" Dash howled, still chuckling. "That's a dirty 'fing to do!"

The classroom doorway filled with a beastly silhouette.

The obese creature's cry was guttural. Demonic. Ear-shattering.

Anthony slipped on the slick, wet surface and smashed onto the floor in a bruising heap. He howled in pain, unsure if he'd broken bones in the fall.

"Stuart, what's the over-under?" Dr. Angus, now inside the booth, nudged Stuart aside to better view the larger screens with her intense eyes.

"Ten minutes."

"What are we at?"

He scoffed. "Four minutes fifteen seconds."

"Can I put twenty on the under? Kid's not even armed yet. Won't even make it to the second creature."

"Bets are closed," Dash smiled.

Blood pounded like angry ocean waves in Anthony's strapped, prodded head.

Toothy approached, slamming his fat feet across the checkered floor into the moonlight. His skin was gray. Slimy. Anthony could see him better now. His slovenly fat folds. His grizzly body was peppered with moles and warts and mangy sprigs of greasy hair. He easily weighed over 500 pounds. A sumo-like slab of greasy flab piled atop a revolting mutant frame.

His eyes were jet-black balls tucked into oversized, puffy sockets. They weren't seated right, one sliding nearly off his face like some off-brand Toxic Avenger.

But the fangs…

His fangs were what nightmares were made of.

Hundreds of them. Long, narrow teeth the length of human fingers, each pierced painfully into his agitated, stinking gums.

Five neat rows.

Like elongated shark teeth.

His jaw clicked open, maw widening like some sort of feeding reptile. Five more sets of serrated ivories on the bottom row. He slammed the jaw closed with raw power. The rotten fangs clicked and crunched against each other.

Anthony screamed. The beast was finished inspiring terror.

Feeding time.

It beelined for Anthony. Faster than its tubby body should be able to move. Toothy pounded through the classroom. Hurled an overturned desk at the wall, shattering it into warped metal and splinters upon impact.

He neared his prey. Anthony was speechless. He plucked a vicious-looking shard of glass from the rodent tank near his head.

He stood, though it pained him, and slashed at Toothy.

Once.

Twice.

The glass whooshed through the air a third time and connected, narrowly missing Toothy's throat, gashing open one of his massive shoulders instead. Gangrenous pus oozed from the malodorous wound in place of blood.

The testers grimaced at the monitors.

Stuart leaned in, anticipation mounting. "Ooof, mate, now you've just pissed it off!"

The creature lunged and slung both putrid, beefy arms around Anthony's shaking knees, crushing them with brute strength before burying all five rows of unhinged fangs into his throat and shoulders. Ripping. Shredding. Jaw locked in place. Teeth like sharpened steel gears making quick work of the gamer's body.

On the sterile slab, Anthony erupted in a chilling scream as the in-game lacerations ripped through his very real, strapped-in torso.

Dr. Angus didn't blink, glued to the screen as Anthony shuddered.

Anthony stabbed the hunk of glass into Toothy's back violently with every bit of strength he could muster. He dug the pointed surface deep into layers of putrid skin and blubber.

Muscles tore. Tendons snapped. Arterial blood sprayed from his shredded carotid artery, spurting on every wall of the recently cleaned room.

Anthony's snarls and screams gurgled in his throat, now full of warm, sanguine liquid. Drowning him in his own life's essence.

Dash galloped to the trashcan to wretch.

Toothy shredded on, splattering the patient's room in vibrant red like a Pollock painting. The beast shredded Anthony's paralyzed extremities into a pulsating mess of gore with those teeth... those hideous teeth.

The creature feasted for nearly a full minute, dining on the hardened bones in Anthony's femur, grinding the surrounding meat into a gelatinous pulp beneath the gnarled, twisted, crimson tissue.

Wasted blood and bile spewed everywhere.

Stuart looked up at the clock and sighed. He dug into his wallet, barely affected by the visceral violence and chaos on the other side of the window. He tossed some cash toward his best friend.

"I'da thought more from a bloke wif' that much supposed elite experience." Stuart stood, grateful the blood-curdling screams had ceased. Death hung heavy in the air. Another eviscerated carcass sat. Unmoving. Ready for disposal.

A final cardinal-red pint trickled out of what was left of Anthony's thighs, and Stuart stretched remorselessly with a squeal, his lanky arms clasped high overhead.

Green. About to be sick again, Dash peered over the rancid contents of the trash can, which were still preferable to the mess beyond the window.

"C'mon, mate," Stuart held out a hand to help him up. "Cleanup time, bruv. Do it fa' the birds in Wayfair." His smile was soft, almost apologetic. "484 comes in at four o'clock."

THE RICTUS GRIN

"Hi, I'm your host, Terry Bates, and this is *Demolition Flicker...*" Terry groaned and acted like he was going to furiously hit the front door with his hammer, pulling back at the last second, "Matt, can we cut?"

"Why? What's wrong?" Matt's near-black eyes peered out from behind the pricey camera, rigged with various gadgets, including an LED monitor and mounted shotgun mic sleeved in its fur cover.

"I said fuckin' 'flicker' and not 'flipper.' Didn't you hear me? You're supposed to be paying attention to that shit." Terry out, voice bellowing through the sunny, serene neighborhood. Beyond him was a picturesque suburban landscape, idyllic and quiet. The leaves of fruit trees glittered in the gentle breeze.

"Sorry, man, normally I have a scripty for that shit." Matt's face contorted into a polite smile, eyes squinting into slits as he waved to a teenager riding by on a noisy bicycle. "Hi."

Matt waved beside the 20mm lens and readjusted the camera's shoulder-mount.

The boy flipped them both off casually and rode on. Matt's smile fell, and he shook his head. "Nice neighborhood. How'd you get this place anyway?"

"Raised a shitload with all the IndieStarter pledges and then got House Junkies to match it as our official sponsor. Then, we started looking around for cheap houses at auction, looking for something that needed like a straight-up demolition."

Matt eyed the house with a look of disgust. "Well, you nailed it."

"Got this place for like *dirt* cheap. $52K, I think. Owners died. They couldn't find the heir. Property was too fucked up for a Realtor to sell, so it went up for auction, and we bought it outright."

Matt sighed deeply, whipped out his phone, pulled up an app, and started looking at the house through it. He flipped through the lens options and decided on the widest. "Okay, I'm thinking six-foot Dana Dolly on full apples with the 18mm lens."

"No, we don't have time for Dana Dolly stuff today. This isn't one of your *avant-garde* stupid indie features. This is a proof-of-concept for television. You know… just run-n-gun."

"Don't hire me for my expertise and then tie my hands, man. Might as well cut my balls off while you're at it."

"Always so dramatic." Terry rolled his eyes and then stared off at the bright sky. Finally, he turned back. "C'mon. Seriously. No Dana Dolly. Shoulder mount or SteadyRig only today. We gotta move fast. Wrecking crew starts tearing it down Monday."

"That's not enough time."

"Yes, it is. It's fine. Let's stop the whining and start the recording. Do you want to have a hit show or not?"

"Hit show?" Matt cackled loudly. "Oh my God, you're fucking serious, aren't you? Holy shit." Matt swung the rig down, dangling it upside down by his thighs with a rippling arm. "You really are taking this that seriously, aren't you?"

"Yes! You should be, too! We have, what, forty-eight hours to shoot this?"

"So? It's never getting picked up. You're doing this dumb shit on spec."

"The people at Nolo want to launch their platform with original content. *Matt, we could be that content!*"

"Is this who you want to be? Some knockoff version of Ty Pennington on the world's next *Crackle*? Come on! With crowdfunding like this, we could have made a feature. Something narrative. Something that means *something* in the world."

"Oh, your little sixty-grand *gems* like *Cannibal Roller Babes?*"

"We won Best Feature in Orlando, we won Best Cinematography in Boulder, we got Best-fucking-Score in Salt Lake City. Some of the fringe Mormons actually loved our shit, dude."

"It's *Cannibal Roller Babes.* Half those women were fuckin' topless through half the movie. You're hardly *Scorsese*, you twat."

"You don't have to be a snob. You think you're Tom Cruise, hosting a reality show, but really you're over here lookin' like..." Matt couldn't find the words. He just motioned to Terry, coming up blank.

"Matt," Terry put his fists on his hips and looked around for a moment before staring right into his eyes, "how fucking *baked* are you right now?"

"Aww, lay off me. What are you, my mother?" Matt rolled his shoulders and groaned. "I'm putting on the SteadyRig. My shoulders are killin' me already."

"Matt, answer the question."

"Terry, you don't want to see me *not* baked, okay?" Matt slid his arms through the holes of the steady rig and clamped the Velcro waistband tight. Overhead, a metal arm reached out at a 90-degree angle over his head. At the end was a retractable tether with a metal claw. He pulled it down, opened the claw, and clamped it securely around the large eye bolt screwed into the casing the camera was surrounded by. He pulled the camera down to chest height, and the tether allowed him slack. He adjusted his focus rings, making sure Terry was sharp.

"I'd love to see you not baked. Especially when we have everything riding on this," Terry grumbled, adjusting his shirt in the reflection of the busted window beside him.

"With as much of a whiny perfectionist as you are, I'd be eating Tums like candy with a bleeding ulcer in my fucking stomach if I had to do this shit sober." Matt sighed and waved a hand sparsely covered in thick, black hair. "Go back to your mark. I'll delete the take, and we'll go again."

"Don't delete the take. Just roll another clip."

"Are you gonna tell me how to do every part of my job? Or are you gonna chill the hell out and remember that I know what the fuck I'm doing? You hired me because I'm *good*."

"No, I hired you because Kim jumped onto that Atlanta Mafia show as a second AC and because Alan's in Tibet shooting some dumb fucking documentary with Kevin McNally."

"Ugh, Kevin's *such* a fucking tool."

"Right?!"

The two stewed in their shared silent hatred for the man for a moment, and then each drew in a long breath to de-escalate.

Finally, Matt spoke again, this time calm. "Sorry, man, I just have a lot riding on this."

"Look, I get it, man. It's fine. Say no more."

"We're burning daylight and need to get this intro in the can."

"You don't say 'in the can' when you're shooting DSLR, Matt. There's nothing to go in a *can*. You don't have to keep acting like we're shooting on film."

Matt patted his hands on his thighs. "Motherfucker, can we shoot this?"

"YES! Jesus Christ!" Terry yowled, voice echoing through the quaint block full of manicured lawns and cookie-cutter houses.

Matt huffed, pressed record, widened his stance, and crouched a few inches while Terry composed himself. He mouthed the intro again to himself, staring at the rotten floorboards beneath him. He re-positioned his feet at the edge of the 'T' made of colorful tape on one of the gnarled planks. The wood groaned uncomfortably beneath him as he looked up into the lens and smiled.

"Hi, I'm Terry Bates, and welcome to *Demolition Flippers*, the show where we buy dilapidated and foreclosed homes, unearth hidden treasures, and then demolish the property so that developers can use the space for attractive new homes that will improve the property values nearby. Today, I am coming to you from Moab, Utah, a town known for its scenic red rock vistas, the Moab Jeep Safari, and a bustling film industry..."

Terry stared at Matt for a moment, eyes blank.

"What?"

"Should we say that?"

"Say what?"

"Bustling film industry?"

"Why wouldn't we? It's true."

"It's *porn*, though. When people ask what kind of films are made in Moab, the answer is porno."

"So? It's not a lie."

"Yeah, but should we be drawing attention to that?"

"You're not." Matt adjusted the focus ring on the camera, double-checking that Terry's eyes were sharp. "If it bothers you, just say the vistas and safari."

"How far up are you seeing on me?"

"It's a medium-wide."

"So, like, thighs up? Why? I was thinking medium or medium-close."

"Because I don't want the hammer to just come out of nowhere like you're some kind of psychopath."

"Oh, copy that."

"Just… relax, man. Let me do the thing I'm good at. You do the thing you're good at."

Terry rolled his neck, giving the bones a solid crack. "Alright, I'm gonna try it again without the porno stuff. How do I look? Hair's alright?" Terry played with his bangs, feeling for stray flyaways, trying to see his reflection in the glare of the rotating polarizer seated in the matte box.

But as Matt glanced at him, something over Terry's shoulder caught his attention.

Something in the far window of the decrepit house they were about to tear apart.

Something tall. Something… *moving*.

It was the height of an adult human but bone-white with dips and curves in all the wrong places, ones that shadowed parts of what would be its face in strange ways. Whatever it was appeared, from his distance, to have too many eyes to be human. The lower half of its face opened, but two black, cavernous pits appeared, though not in unison. It was almost as if the thing had two sets of lower mandibles, each capable of opening or closing one of the orifices individually. Its skin was gaunt and sallow, hollow in spots, and tinged as white as the rows of teeth in both of its mouths…

"What the fuck?!" Matt tripped on his own feet, clamoring in the opposite direction. His sole caught on one of the weather-damaged floorboards, and he slammed onto his back, feeling the metal of the rig smash against his spine with force. The camera shot up on its tether, swinging wildly through the air suspended inches off the ground by the rig. It whipped past his head like a dangerous pendulum on the cable, so close he could feel the rush of air on his face, thankful the careening gear didn't smash his teeth out of their seated holes and into the back of his throat.

Terry scrambled toward the whirling camera, clutching it mid-air like a fragile egg thrown from the roof to stop it from its dangerous path. "Jesus,

Matt! You okay? You almost smashed the camera!"

Terry erupted in a nervous chuckle, panting like someone who just successfully fled the law in a chase. "Thank God you were wearing the steady rig! We'd be fucked!"

But Matt wasn't relieved about the save. He could only stare at the empty back window of the property, black and dead, imagining the disgusting being probably lurking beyond in the darkness. The window was a rectangular void now, like a dark portal to something nightmarish.

"Jesus, Matt. Is it the heat or something? C'mon. Let's go inside and sit you down. I'll get you a cold La Croix from the cooler."

"No," Matt muttered, feeling the strong urge to piss his pants every time the image of that... thing... made its way back into his mind's eye.

The *last* thing he wanted to do was go inside.

***

As the afternoon sun ducked behind the mountainous wall to the shoddy structure's west, Terry sat inside shuffling through mounds of paperwork, newspapers, clothing, old children's toys, and dust-covered miscellaneous garbage.

With great trepidation and roaming eyes, Matt attempted to document Terry's work with his camera, one dangling once again from the stabilization rig strapped to his chest. He could feel his heart race beneath the Velcro and nylon, subtly shaking the jacket's metal-and-plastic exoskeleton. His smartwatch vibrated, startling him. He glanced at it. Due to his elevated pulse, the watch congratulated him for meeting his daily exercise goal.

Unnerved, Matt's focus shot back to the three-inch monitor attached to the camera via a small, jointed black arm. He tried to sound calm and unafraid. "Hey man, let's get a shot of you by the front door doing a walk-in like you're just seeing the place for the first time."

"Yeah, good idea." Terry drew a deep breath and nodded. He waltzed over to the door and adjusted his shirt. "How's the shirt? Do I have anything in my teeth?" He bared his chompers like a smiling dog.

Matt normally would have said something comical in jest, but the image of that *thing* in the window rattled him. "Yeah, man, all good."

Matt still wasn't sure what he'd seen.

It seemed to just be... *lurking* there, shadowy and threatening.

Watching them.

It looked about six feet tall if he had to wager a guess. He couldn't shake the thought that someone was inside the disgusting house with them.

Terry cleared his throat and plastered on a fake grin. "Alright, folks, part of what we like to do here is go through all of the items in a house once we purchase it at auction. You never know what kind of hidden jackpots you'll find in a place like this. It could be trash or treasure. We don't know until we start digging. We're sort of like... archaeologists, unearthing interesting or worthwhile items hidden in plain sight. Many of these items can be sold online, many to antique shops, and others might be donated, up-cycled, or destroyed. But that is part of the *fun* of all of this," he said with a broad, cheesy smile. "We aren't just flipping houses here. We're making something beautiful. We are finding new homes where items will be cherished instead of dumping them all in a landfill. And we are making bank while we're doing it."

As Terry finished his sentence, he hunched down, reached into a lumpy pile of clutter, and pulled out a book of collectible baseball cards, vintage and carefully encased in a plastic sleeve. With his other hand, he pulled out a book of stamps, also in a plastic sleeve. He held them up and smiled for a few awkward seconds.

"Aaaand, cut." Matt rubbed his goatee with one hand. "I don't know, Terry. I don't know if anyone's going to buy that someone who keeps a shithole like this is gonna actually have their collectibles ."

Terry straightened his legs to stand. "Matt, I'm not fucking sticking my bare cards in that pile. These are fucking mint. They're worth more than we raised crowdfunding for this fucking pilot."

"I'm just saying it feels a bit staged, is all. It's just a bit... convenient."

Just then, the men heard scuffling from the next room, like an animal nesting. But whatever made the sound was much too large just to be a rodent.

"Oh Jesus, was that a fucking rat?" Terry asked.

Matt remained quiet. He wouldn't have guessed rats. He would have guessed that fucking six-foot nightmare with two sets of teeth he'd seen earlier...

"This place has been dilapidated for a long time. Probably a shitload of raccoons and stuff living in here. We've gotta be careful."

"I just wanna be fucking *done* today," Matt growled. "I just wanna go back to the hotel, relax, and have a beer."

"Let's just get through this, and then we can chill and offload." Terry shook his head. "What do you want me to do? Do you want to re-shoot it? I don't wanna take the cards out of the sleeve. These are worth a lot of money, and this place is gross."

"Well, if that's the case, look around. Is there something in this fucking mess that is actually worth a piss that you can use for real?"

"Probably not. I can check."

"You check, and I'll film you rooting around in here for some fun B-roll later. We need a bunch of it. I'll just let it roll for a few."

Terry sighed and looked at the heaps around him. "Fine. I don't know where the hell to start, honestly."

"Start where you are now, and I'll just follow you. But, maybe put a little, you know, urgency in it because there are still a few more things on the shot list to do before we can wrap for the night."

"Copy that." Terry was miles away already, shuffling through a dusty file of paperwork in a tattered folio. "Can I talk during this part, or should I just look like I'm investigating?"

"I wouldn't talk. It's gonna look weird in the edit if you do since you don't have an assistant or anything on screen."

"Yeah, true."

Matt twisted the follow-focus knob on the side of the camera, sharpening Terry's image. He crab-walked in a semi-circle around Terry, capturing a smooth shot of the man hard at work.

Terry looked concerned.

"Maybe try not to look like you're dropping a painful deuce."

"Sorry." Terry shook his head as if he didn't believe his eyes. "This is like some sort of medical document. This dude was *seriously* fucked up. Tons of like… abnormalities and birth defects." He looked at the outer label on the patient folder and blew the dust off of it. He squinted and mumbled it aloud. "Jones, Ronald."

"It ain't all gonna be treasure in there." Matt shivered.

Everything about this rotten piece of termite-infested property gave him the creeps.

Terry peeled back some more papers and grimaced at his findings. "Patient's deformities are severe. Two sets of eyes. Two full, working mandibles. Suffers from *rictus sardonicus*, the sustained abnormal spasm during which facial muscles appear to be grinning, also known as a *rictus grin*." He squinted harder to read the doctor's writing. "Ewww. The patient's mother and father were *siblings…* shit, an incest twist? Now we finally have a real hook for the studio."

Despite Terry's sorry attempt at a joke, Matt wasn't laughing. The words that had just come from his friend's mouth chilled his blood into an iced sludge. What the file had described felt *eerily similar* to what he'd seen in the window less than an hour before. Two individual, hideous mouths made for spewing and gnawing… four unblinking eyes made for that maniacal, thousand-yard stare… and that sallow, ungodly skin, barely sheathing the collection of hardened bones beneath.

Could he still be…

No, Matt shook his head, *don't even go there.*

Just then, through the silence came a scratching sound. The sound of small legs and claws scrabbling through the mess around them.

"Jesus, what the hell *is* that?" He held up his hands in the shape of a 'T' for a timeout. Terry nodded. Matt unclipped the camera and set it on a wicker chair, barely held together, wood gouged with claw marks.

The scuffling grew louder. Matt whipped around again, expecting the piles to start writhing above the swift, rodent army he was imagining. He pulled out the multi-tool in his front jeans pocket and unfurled the small blade from it. He held the bulky thing defensively.

Terry laughed. "You look ridiculous right now. What are you gonna do? Stab a rat if it comes at you?"

"You're goddamn *right,* I am!" Matt clomped through the tight clearing beneath boxes and furniture toward what he imagined was the kitchen.

The roof was half caved-in in one corner, allowing the dank room to be illuminated by nature's skylight. The red blotch of Utah sunset looked like a raw, picked scab on the otherwise dingy ceiling.

More scratching. Nails on wood and the slow, heavy thump of something beyond the kitchen door.

Matt held his pocketknife out, watching the thin strip of sharpened metal shake in his bracelet-riddled arm. The beads of his loose-fitting obsidian band clicked together.

"Hello? Someone in here?"

"Yeah, *me,* you dickweed!" Terry snickered.

Matt pressed his chapped lips into a line, flustered, cursing Terry in his mind as he edged closer to the closed door at the other end of the kitchen.

Something moved in his periphery. A dusty box of cereal inched itself across the counter. He turned to it, heart beating in his chest.

A , brown rat yanked its head from the box, holding a piece of cereal between its long, yellow teeth. It stared at him, sizing him up.

"You little…" He stepped forward to grab something to throw at the critter, but his foot landed on something soft and yielding.

SQUEAK!

The earth was alive and moving beneath his worn sole. The lump beneath his foot squeezed out with resiliency, and Matt lost his balance. He lurched forward at the counter. The rat dropped his cornflake and shot forward like a dart. It grappled on his messy wad of dyed-black hair using its strong, tiny hands to clench tight. In a flurry of scrambling legs, the animal used his scalp as a launch pad to jet off, airborne into the darkened depths of the room like a skydiver without a chute.

Another rat scuttled over his gouged leather sneaker. Matt shrieked. The noise brought two more out of an open bag of dry dog food, dusty and crinkling beneath their hefty weight. They scuttled off, tails slithering behind like hairy snakes.

"Fuck... this!" Matt's voice was shrill as he stormed out of the kitchen. He snatched up his camera and shot out the front door. "I'm fuckin' outtie, Ter."

"What? Wait, Matt, where are you going?"

"Back to the hotel."

Terry followed him out to the overgrown front yard, loaded with tufts of tall grass and out-of-control weeds. "Matt, what'd you see back there?!"

"Rats, dude. A whole bunch of 'em!" Matt popped the trunk of his SUV, opened his Porta-brace bag, and stuffed the camera inside. He ripped the Velcro and clips from his vest open and let the metal-and-fabric SteadyRig fall flat on the asphalt behind him. He braced himself on his taillights and leaned into the trunk, chewing his bottom lip nervously.

"Hey. Matt. Talk to me."

Finally, he turned to look at Terry. "I'll make some calls tonight. I'll try to find you another DP, okay? I just... I can't go back in there."

"You're gonna let all this little shit ruin your payday, Matt?" Terry grabbed the man's arm, trying desperately to connect eyes with him. "Come on. I know you need the money. Sarah told me about the house."

"She *what?*"

"She told me about the bank… threatening the foreclosure. I was throwin' you a *bone* with this gig."

"Awww, goddammit, man. She's got a big fucking mouth."

"Of course, she told me, man. We are friends. We've known each other back since the second season of *American Scream Queen.* Back when she was just a wardrobe PA. She and I go way back like car seats. Of *course,* she was gonna tell me!"

"It's all the damned strikes, man. They just dragged that shit out. We've been living on savings for, like, damn near nine months."

"I know. We're *all* hurtin'." Then, Terry frowned. "I know about the… *other* thing, too."

"What other thing?"

"Dude, come on." Terry just stared into his eyes like an upset parent.

"What?"

"I know… before the strikes, you weren't just day-playing on *Morrowvale.* I know you got fired from the show."

"Oh, Jesus! Is there anything Sarah *didn't* fuckin' blab about?"

"Sarah didn't tell me that. Jared, one of the set PAs, *he* messaged me the day it happened."

"Is he that lanky little asshole with the poodle hair?"

Terry chuckled. "Yeah. He said he was helping the crafty guy move a table out of the fire lane by you when it happened."

"Ugh… seriously?" Matt groaned and let his head flop back.

"Yeah. He told me all about your blowout with the 1st AC. Said you called the guy a cunt."

"That guy *is* a cunt. Goddamned ancient-ass focus-puller was trying to make me be his little errand bitch. Making me fetch him chips and shit all the time 'cause he's got old-ass knees. Motherfucker's *lazy's* what it is."

Terry grabbed Matt's biceps and stared into his face. "Look, I get it. It is what it is. You're like a cat, man. You have nine lives with this kinda stuff. You'll bounce back and be on some fucking Tier-1 Hulu gig next month. I *get* that. But right now, you have a chance to keep the bank from selling your house while you're *in* it." Terry smiled a little. "It's just rats, man. Just overgrown mice. They can't maim you. They're just gross."

"One was in my hair, man! It latched onto me."

"Hey! Focus up," Terry barked. "Keep your eyes on the prize. Get back inside and finish this day strong, and I'll buy you a twelve-pack of Blue Moon and a pizza on the way back to the hotel. My treat."

After a long, tense moment, Matt grumbled, "Better be fucking pepperoni. None of this *plain cheese* bullshit."

"Copy that. Pepperoni pizza and beer for second meal." Terry nodded. A smile crept onto his pensive face.

Matt yanked the camera back out of its felt-lined coffin and sighed hard and heavy. "Fine."

***

Matt's camera was speeding on a take of Terry shuffling through the home. "Narrate what you're doing as you go. You don't want the episode to seem like a silent film."

"Okay. Is my lav showing? I feel like it keeps peeking out the front of my shirt." Terry pointed to the area between his pecs where the mic had been taped to his skin beneath the fabric.

"No, mic looks good. Can't see it. But hold up a sec." Matt traipsed over to an LED panel light casting its blue-tinged glow on the horrid wallpaper and adjusted the dial on the back with his free hand. He kicked the base of the metal C-stand it was mounted atop until the unit was even with Terry.

Terry held up a pile of X-rays. The layers were stuck together, peeling apart loudly like something tacky and adhesive. Terry's face turned sour at the noise. "Ewwww."

"What is it?"

"Our incest freak's scans. Oh my God, this guy was like something out of *The Hills Have Eyes*." Terry shivered dramatically. He held up one of the X-rays toward the panel light and grimaced at the gnarled skull in the image. "Jones, Ronald."

The X-rays were a winding road map of bony irregularities

As Matt started back into position, his eyes locked onto something in the next room. A wraith-like form, spindly and narrow. Taller than Terry.

The crimson sunset oozed through the thick curtains behind it, making it look like a demon. Frozen in plain sight. Looming and imposing...

"There it is again!"

Terry whirled around, and the thing stood stone-still.

"What is that? Please tell me that that's like some kind of cigar store Indian or something! What a find that would be."

Terry started through the darkened doorway toward it.

"Don't!"

"That would be worth a pretty penny!"

"Terry, for fuck's sake! That isn't a statue!"

"I just wanna see what it is. Roll the camera. I don't want to have to fake this reaction again if it's something good."

"Jesus Christ, stop!"

Terry ignored him, reaching into his back pocket and fishing out his cell phone. He illuminated the torch on it, sweeping the flashlight through the darkness.

The beam brushed across a rickety brass bed, rumpled and broken with a mattress splattered in bile and excrement. Brown hand prints marked up the walls, reeking of once-liquefied stool and dried blood. Beheaded toys and half-gnawed rat carcasses littered the floor.

Terry's light finally settled on the thing before him, and his smile washed away like initials beneath a lapping wave.

"What... the fuck... is that?"

Light lit up a pair of blinding white legs that looked like a bundle of bones wrapped tightly in a latex sheet. Sparse leg hair gave way to a thick thatch of unkempt pubic hair and a dangling, uncircumcised dick. Above it were ribs like two xylophones reaching up to a pair of long, blinding arms.

It moved, taking a single, long stride closer to Terry. He dropped his phone and hunched fast, scrambling to find it among the sea of tails and tiny legs among the ass-ends of an army of shorn rodents.

He lifted the light again, this time to the being's face, wishing instantly that he hadn't.

The man, if one could call him that, gnawed rodent entrails with his lower mouth and then raised what remained of the rat to the higher mouth, shoving it between two more sets of gnashing teeth until it ripped off the animal's leg. The vicious bottom mouth swallowed and seized into a smile. The second mouth followed suit, peeling its lips back and baring its teeth as if convulsing beneath a slow electric current.

Terry's light rose higher still, all of this instantly set to the soundtrack of his pounding pulse in his throat. The man before him opened his bottom set of eyes and then the top set, staring at Terry with all four.

Like food...

"Is that... Ronald?" Matt yelled, voice warbling with fear.

The man's tendonous claw tossed the rat's remains into a corner, and he opened both sets of jaws wide and hissed from both in unison.

"*Huuuuun-gyyy*," the jaws crowed.

Terry screamed, then Matt from afar.

The creature lumbered forward, swiping at Terry. He turned to run and started out of the room, squishing soft remains of long-discarded rodents with his racing feet. His foot caught on some jutting wood in the threshold, and Terry took a hard spill into the kitchen.

Matt moved for him, but the sight of the nearing... thing... made him back away, camera swinging wild from the SteadyRig cable attached over his head. It bashed into the light, then the cabinet, and Terry slipped on some newsprint, grasped for the C-stand, and clattered to the floor along with the footed metal pole.

Just as Terry stood, Matt watched the nude, skeletal man reach overhead and yank off a plank of rotten wood from the rickety door jamb. He looked down at it, long nails still jutting out of the end of it. As Terry stood, the man lifted the wood overhead like a club and swung it down hard, burying both nails inches into Terry's skull. Matt watched, close enough to touch him, as Terry's eyes rolled back in his head, mouth widening in a silent scream.

The man thrashed the wood backward, taking Terry with it and dropping him to the floor. He pressed a bare foot to Terry's throat, one with long, yellowed toenails that glowed in the light of the overturned panel light.

"No!" Matt screamed.

CRACK!

The man stomped hard on Terry's neck, breaking the fragile vertebral bones beneath in an instant under the weight of his tall, slight figure.

With Terry stilled, Matt scrambled away backward like a crab, stuck in his camera rig, dodging the heavy, swinging weight of the RED camera and all of its accouterments at the end of the sturdy tether.

The man swung the board sideways like a bat at Matt but missed and buried the nails deep into the cupboard door beneath the dingy kitchen sink, heaped with shattered dishware and buzzing flies.

"*Huuuuun-gyyy,*" the inbred creep mewled again.

Matt's eyes widened so much at the feel of the air from the near-hit that he thought his orbital sockets might tear in the corners.

Matt made one final attempt to flee, but the man was on him, leaping like a wild dog and slamming the cameraman to the floor.

In a flash, the man wrapped the camera's tether around Matt's throat and pulled hard with the camera, cinching his throat in like a noose. The man's pleading face turned purple quickly.

Matt heard laughter, two separate voices, like a diabolical echo, bouncing off the narrow walls of the filthy space around them, both coming from the twin orifices in front of him.

The man pulled tighter, wrenching the tether like a garrote around Matt's throat. He raised the camera a few feet over Matt's maroon face.

Before his skull was reduced to a mash of gnarled meat, smashed brains, and busted circuitry, Matt saw four eyes blink.

Two mouths were frozen in a fixed grin as both of Ronald's muddled voices cooed, "*Huuuuun-gyyy*" in near-unison one final time.

AUTHOR'S NOTES

TINES: This was originally published in Eerie River's Anthology called It Calls From Below. I'm not 100% sure what possessed me to write this one. I can say that it was an amalgamation of things that I loved from several works I've read and seen. The wormy/viral element was inspired by a combination of the underrated 2005 film Isolation (starring Ruth Negga, who I fangirled over later when we worked together on a television show called Preacher for several seasons) and an even more underrated film called Impulse (starring Tim Matheson and Meg Tilly in 1984) that I saw at a formative age.

I had also read Ian Reid's I'm Thinking of Ending Things about a year prior and found the family in it to be so eerie and unsettling.

I loosely based the girl's mother off of my own, including a few things my mother used to say on a loop, almost verbatim, and loosely based the daughter on my angsty younger self.

The voice in the ground was inspired by one of my mother's many mental illnesses. It was often difficult growing up to ascertain whether

271

she was being paranoid or really experiencing strange occurrences all the time, especially because I'm not a terribly observant person. (Ironic for a writer, I know)

I wanted the voice to be something people discuss after the story is over.

Is the voice in the hole real? Or is it a byproduct of the illness they've all gotten from eating the tainted food from the farm? I have my own theories, but I wanted to leave it up to the reader to decide and discuss.

This is still one of my favorite stories that I've ever written.

***

DERAILED: For this story, I wanted to tap into two very real fears of mine, traumas that have caused me moderate cases of PTSD:

The first was my car accident in 2020, depicted from pretty much my exact point of view in this story, with only a few minor details changed. I was moving up to Connecticut with my boyfriend Dave and he witnessed the whole thing from the rear-view mirror of the U-haul truck full of all my belongings. He saw me and our two Jack Russels flip in my CR-V off the side of the road in Alabama after a sudden blown tire (one less than a year old). He watched me nearly get T-boned by a semi, fly off the road, flip upside down, and careen into a ditch where the dogs and I were crushed upside-down inside a four-wheeled, metal tomb where I nearly suffocated to death on the seat belt that also saved my life and kept me from being decapitated instantly.

It was the most harrowing experience of my life, on par with the cancer I had at 19 that had doctors forcing me to plan my own funeral.

Perhaps even more wild than the accident was the fact that the dogs and I and Dave all walked away from the scene with just a few minor cuts, one bump on the head, one shredded tongue, and a bundle of PTSD. So much so that I would later have a panic attack in a movie theater with friends while watching the upside-down car chase in Christopher Nolan's Tenet.

I remember the accident so vividly that, ever since, I thought: I have to put this in a story.

Secondly, I had a very mentally ill mother growing up. She was diagnosed with several serious mental illnesses and later went undiagnosed, with likely even more.

After her involuntary stay at a mental institution, she somehow went largely unmedicated for the decades to come. It is my opinion that her passive husband exacerbated her issues, creating a toxic echo chamber that left/leaves her wholly unchecked.

Though I could write wild volumes about it all (she's given me enough trauma for an entire career as an author of extreme horror,) she IS still alive. I imagine her antics haven't slowed (like hitchhiking two hours south to Tampa to live in a tent on the sidewalk for a week outside of Best Buy on an enraged whim or putting pieces of our dead family ferret in the refrigerator to try to Google scientists willing to clone it. True story.)

But I don't want to say anything here that will give her any reason to reach out after I've excommunicated her for well over a decade. It was the best decision that I have ever made for my own mental health, and my life improved drastically after doing so.

While she never thought I was a rat, there was lots of talk in my childhood home (a home that producers of the show "Extreme Hoarders" said they wanted to use as the season finale after I submitted pictures to the show) about the government sending roaches with built-in listening devices like walking wire-taps (I remember watching her hose the house down with RAID roach spray. Telephone receivers, silverware, plates…) and her having us don foil hats in the house around the time the movie Signs came out.

Derailed is a tale where I tackle two genuine fears: What would have happened if I had been maimed in that horrific accident? And what do I truly think would happen if I had to go live at my mother's house right now, allowing her to take care of me after she's gone unchecked and unhinged for so long?

This story is the marriage of those two chilling ideas.

***

PAINTED IN VERMILLION: A few years ago, when I lived in Louisiana, I took a weekend trip to Lafayette a couple hours away with my ex-boyfriend, Anthony, (the garbage-human who inspired the story Feed the Machine, which I will discuss shortly), and my friends Ashley, Jeremy, and Rebecca. We loaded up the kayaks and coolers and fishing rods, rented a cabin, and thought we'd spend a relaxing weekend on the water and forget all of our troubles.

Though the trip was fun, it was loaded with drama (mostly because of my ex, who gave himself a nearly emergency-room-level sunburn kayaking and then spent the rest of the weekend whining and picking fights with everyone.)

At one point, Rebecca and I decided to escape for a bit and go up the river apiece on the kayaks for a lazy trek.

Our excursion was horrific.

About a mile or so upriver, the sky darkened. I thought it was a rain cloud or something at first (as I mentioned earlier, for a writer, I am oddly not very observant sometimes.) Within seconds, we realized it was a swarm of something... living. We started paddling and a moment later, we were being smacked with these huge, hideous, grasshopper or dragonfly-looking bugs.

We screamed bloody-effing-murder, which was a mistake because several took that opportunity to fly inside my mouth.

I had no idea if these things were biters or poisonous... or what the hell they were. We only knew there were literally millions of them upon us.

After about 60 seconds of sheer hell, it was over. The insect-cyclone passed, and we were no longer in the eye of the storm. I looked around to see a sea of these bugs. Some dead in trees like leaves, some in my hair, a layer of their corpses littering our kayaks, and the million that had committed some sort of instant kamikaze suicide into the water.

I checked for bites, and Rebecca did the same. I believe we might have even been full blubber-crying at this point, looking like total wussies.

I said at one point, "Ashley is smart. She will know exactly what these are if I take one back."

We headed straight back to the cabin, hearts still racing. Once there, I show Ashley this bug that I'm carrying like it's the only proof that I'm not bat-shit crazy (even though some are still in my hair and clothes)

Ashley buckles with laughter, barely able to get out the information to us that the bugs were just mayflies. They don't have mouths. They spawn, breed, and basically commit suicide in a several-hour span every year. We just so happened to be there on 'the day.'

Years later, Eerie River Publishing called for Air-related horror stories, and that experience came to mind. I thought to myself... but what if they did have mouths? What if they were nefarious creatures? And the story flowed from there.

Also, the title, Painted in Vermilion, comes from a Phish song that my boyfriend, Dave, loves.

I decided to weave it into the tale since I made the swarm colorful.

***

SATED: This is one of the dearest to my heart in this collection. While it may not be my favorite in terms of content, it is one of my favorites in terms of where the story stems from.

At five years old, my mother and father had a Wang computer with a Tandy monitor and a dot-matrix printer (I still miss peeling those brad holes off both sides of the accordioned printouts!) The computer only had DOS mode, which for those of you too young to remember, it was basically a black screen where you could type, give basic functions, and use the computer as a word processor, basically.

At five, I come up from our computer room (an unfinished room the size of a small bathroom in our dank basement decorated with wall-to-wall horror books, faux candelabras, fake skulls, and anything demonic-looking my mom could get her hands on) with a five-page story called Restaurant of Blood.

My horror-loving parents beamed with pride as I read them my shoddy little tale about a restaurateur who kills a mean man and serves him as steaks in his failing establishment but people love the steaks so much and the demand becomes so high that he is forced to keep killing townspeople to keep the business open.

Last year there was a call for flash fiction that I wanted to enter, and one of the themes was 'cannibalism,' so I thought, how cool would it be if I went back to my roots and re-wrote that very first story I ever wrote in my life with the skills I have now.

It was a lot of fun to write, and brought me great joy to see how far I'd come as a writer in those 30-plus years.

***

IN THE BLOOD OF THE MARTYR: Most who know me, know I had a pretty horrific and tumultuous childhood. While this story is clearly about a young female raped and/or molested (whatever Rorschach your brain wanted you to see) I must say this was one of the only things I did not endure as a kid (I am so thankful about that to this day because there were many shitty people in our lives who had the motive, means, and opportunity to do so) so that part of this tragic-yet-hopeful tale was totally made up.

The part that was not made up was the Pentecostal church which was an amalgamation of several churches I attended as a child (set in some fictional New England town. If you thought it had a Silent Hill vibe to it, then I aced my side-goal. Achievement unlocked... hopefully!)

My grandmother, Nina, no correlation to the Nina in the story (oh, my God, I couldn't even type that lie with a straight face. It's definitely her and if she were still alive she'd be pretty angry about this whole story in general but she was kind of a jerk so, grandma, you had this one a-comin'!) was a pretty hardcore Pentecostal. Since we spent a lot of time together in my youngest years of life, I therefore became Pentecostal by default. When you're young, you believe anything.

I said my many daily prayers in tongues to keep the devil from listening in. I've handled snakes and convulsed in aisles, arms outstretched, singing my ass off. I've seen "miracle" faith healing. People in wheelchairs learning to walk through the "power of Christ" and hefty whack to the ol' noggin.

All of that, in this story, is real.

I found out one day the very hard way (after getting kicked out of a friends Catholic church service) that not all religions behave that way and became rapidly disenchanted with everything I'd been a part of to that point.

While we didn't have baptisms of blood, I still saw a lot of wild stuff in the years I attended. I'm not Pentecostal now (if it isn't already very obvious) or even really "religious," but Pentecostalism is on "the list" I have of things that scare the crap out of me that I use for the inspiration for my stories. I wrote this story about it, just in case it scares others the same way it freaks me out.

***

ALL THE SAME COLOR ON THE INSIDE: Sometimes my union work sends me gigs as a stagehand for concerts and I meet the most bizarre people in my travels. One of these people, I work with regularly so I won't say his real name (this elderly man is absolutely infatuated with me and firmly believes "one day I will be his girl" despite the fact that he is old enough to be my grandfather.)

This man has a sweet and charming side (the huggy, here let me give you one of the caramels in my pocket side) and also a very skeevy, unsettling sexist and racist side. He's tiny. He only comes up to my armpit.

One day I was considering ideas to explore for another flash fiction anthology that was open for stories. This man said something very blatantly racist to me about one of the Black men on our work team and I got upset over it. So the next day, I wrote this story about him getting his just desserts for being a racist.

Also, I was super into Lor Gislason's work at the time (author of Inside Out) and I was determined to be a part of the 'goop horror' sub-genre I was sure that was just starting to take hold.

A year later, it still hasn't really become as popular as I'd hoped, but I like to dabble in different sub-genres and I did get to try my hand at the concept which I'm proud of.

***

SECONDHAND KISS: There isn't much of a clever or insightful backstory to this one. I just really wanted to try my hand at cosmic horror to see if I had any skill at it. I was really missing the Anterim Coast and the friends I made during a film festival years ago in Northern Ireland (George, Kenny, & Roddy especially) and I was obsessed with the way Yale (which is like a five minute drive from my house) looks in the fall.

Secondhand Kiss was my way of blending all of those concepts into something fun and entertaining and slightly angsty & romantic.

***

TAKE A BREATH: This story was my first story to ever be released through another press. (Two Lip Garden was the first to technically be published but the book never came out and the publishing house went under before anyone got any copies.)

The idea for this story came to me when my boyfriend, Dave, was teaching me to surf in Narragansett, Rhode Island a couple years ago. I bought a beginner board and a shitty wetsuit and took a couple days worth of lessons from him.

Dave has been an avid surfer his entire adult life. It's one of his passions and I can totally see why. It's a lot of fun and unlike anything I've ever done.

The only downside is (other than super sore muscles the next day and sand in your crack) is that surfing can be super-freaking-dangerous. Besides pulled muscles and bruising, there are a myriad of ways to get hurt while surfing. There's drowning, being sliced open by the bottom fin of your own board or someone else's (surfers often cluster and there is no way to know their skill level by just looking at them. I nearly cut a kid with my own fin on the day I was learning.) There are also rocks beneath, tumultuous weather, undertows, riptides, sharks…

So choosing it as a setting for a horror story was an easy choice.

Since surfing is often a sport or hobby you want to do alone (it sucks to get to a good surf spot and see a million people fighting over the same spot) I paired it with themes of intense loneliness, hopelessness, and suicide.

To top it all off, I made the idyllic ocean setting the real villain of the story.

The version published here is slightly different from the one published in Hellbound Book's Anthology of Splatterpunk in that I added a siren element to it. While the story worked great without it, I have always had an affinity for the concept of sirens and thought that the imagery added a little edge of freakiness to an already gruesome story.

***

TWO LIP GARDEN: This story was originally under contract to be published in an anthology. The publishers asked me to change the title to The Mother, which I did, because I didn't want to chance getting turned down for my very first paid story. Their company quietly went bankrupt and the book was never released. I never saw a copy of it. I am so glad it is finally being released in this collection.

This story explores one of my all-time favorite hobbies and one of my absolute worst fears. The hobby is gardening. Anyone who knows me, knows I basically tend to a tiny farm wherever I live. I am always giving away bags of surplus tomatoes and peppers or zucchini as big as your calf.

I have always loved the song Gardening at Night by R.E.M. and in Louisiana, after my divorce from my ex-husband, Carl, I decided to spend some of my waking insomnia-filled hours with a little shop light in the back yard, tending to my veggie garden in the otherwise pitch-black night. I loved it. It was so quiet and peaceful (the only downside was that the lights drew bugs and the bugs drew a lot of bats so I was constantly getting freaked out by cruising bats getting a little too close for comfort.) But, I cannot recommend night-gardening enough for you night owls out there!

The fear I explored is memory loss. This is something I really struggle with personally. Childhood traumas have really hampered my memory in a troublesome way (to the point where I couldn't even remember what happens in half of these stories that I wrote until I re-read them for this publication, all of which have been written in the last two years.) On top of already not being able to keep details straight and remember things, I have had family members with dementia and seeing them lose their memory scares the absolute shit out of me.

So this is a story about a woman experiencing that dementia, longing for that familial bond she vaguely remembers once having, while gardening at night.

***

FEED THE MACHINE: This was a fun one that surprisingly became my very first title ever to hit 100 reviews on Amazon (Goodreads, too) which shocks me every time I think about it. After all, my first novel Mantis has received glowing praise and was published in 2016 and yet, at the time of this printing, only has nine reviews. So the attention this story has gotten has blown my mind. Also at conventions, people come up to me and tell me all the time that this story got them to take a chance on my other work. To anyone who has already read it or only bought this collection to have that story in print, I thank you from the bottom of my heart.

This story was inspired by a few things. The first, I centered it around two cheeky Brits with a long history. Stuart and Dash are two actual people I met in real life. They were roadies at a Roger Waters concert I worked and they were my bosses for the day. They had me laughing until I cried by lunchtime and when the call came for an anthology called No Lives Left about video game horror, I knew these two would make such good characters to base the story around.

…So for the people who left reviews saying that Dash is not a real name in the UK, I'd like to let you know he is a real person and you can find him wherever the Roger Waters tour is right now.

Another inspiration for this story was the aforementioned ex-boyfriend who thought he was God's gift to gaming. He worked at EA Games for a few months and spent a lot of money at Gamestop and thought he was the pillar of knowledge on the subject, to the point that whenever someone would mention the word game he would make sure they knew to praise him as their Lord and savior. I saw many people flash him glances like they wanted to beat him to a pulp with a 2x4 over this subject so I, of course, had to get out my (and their) myriad of frustrations through this gory little story.

He is the worst person I've ever known in my life (and I've known some super-shitty people and had a pretty screwed-up home life growing up so that's saying something) and it only seemed fitting that he would inspire such a gruesome fictional demise.

While I knew from the start that I wanted to go full-splatterpunk with this tale, I knew with Stuart and Dash involved, it had to also have some black comedy. So I gave the plot a little bit of a Cabin in the Woods vibe with the people in charge acting like this stuff is all just 'the norm.'

***

THE RICTUS GRIN: This story was inspired by the cover, actually (I know, I know… it sounds like such a backwards way to do things.)

Sometime last year, Rooster Republic Press was having a holiday sale on some of their pre-made covers and while searching around, I found this cover image and fell instantly head-over-heels in love with it. I told my sister right away that I wanted to do something with it because it's just so creepy. Originally, it was going to be the cover to a standalone novella sometime a year or two in the future. I was going to call it Rictus. Or The Rictus Grin.

Then, months later, I decided I wanted to put out a collection in May once my contracts were up on some of these stories and it all just sort of clicked into place that I could use it as the cover for the collection and write a story instead of a novella for The Rictus Grin.

The idea was sort of a loose homage to a film that terrified me as a child called Bad Ronald, about a man who secretly lived in the walls of a suburban home and spied on the family that bought the house next. I knew I wanted to do my own version of that.

Then, later when talking about my idea with JP Behrens at a convention, he gave me the idea to have a man go through items in the house to sort of reveal information about the man secretly living in it. It was then that the idea also popped into my head to make it a reality house-flipping type show.

I had also just watched the limited series, The Curse, fairly recently and found it wildly entertaining. I'm sure that subconsciously played into my decision to set this all during a proof-of-concept/pilot.

I have worked in the film industry for well over a decade so I thought it would be fun to work the equipment and lingo and behavior of some of the low-budget shit shows I've worked on in between huge TV shows and films.

I thought this was a fun way of sort of combining my film background with my fear of a Bad Ronald phrogger (the term "phrogging" didn't exist in the Bad Ronald days to my knowledge but it gives one of my worst nightmares an official title.)

SPECIAL THANKS

I would like to thank a few people who made *The Rictus Grin and Other Tales of Insanity* possible:

To Heather Wohl, my she-ro, my sister, and my partner in crime. I would be absolutely lost without you.

To Chisto Healy, one of my best friends in the business. Thank you for *everything*, man!

To my friends and fellow (extremely talented) authors, JP Behrens and Angel Van Atta for the blurbs on the wrap.

To Mark Anthony and David-Jack Fletcher, the editors of several of these stories. Thank you both for your talent, time, and for being amazing men.

To Rooster Republic Press for the inspiring cover art.

To Ash Ericmore, Otis Bateman, Stephen Cooper, I love you guys. To Mia Faller, John Ryland, Justin Boote, Amber Upson, Eric Butler, Mick Collins, Erica Wetzel-Fields, Corrina Morse, Asher Dark, Eve Bullet, Splatter-Axe Mike, Mort Stone, Wrath James White, Aron Beauregard, Adam Cesare, Corrina Morse, and

291

all of the amazing people who support me, share my posts, read my work, inspire me, or are just plain kind to me…

Thank you for being who you are.

And, lastly, to Dave. *My sun, my moon, my stars.* Thank you for sincerely supporting me in every aspect of my crazy creative journey through this life.

ABOUT THE AUTHOR

Erica Summers is an independent filmmaker, artist, film industry grip, and writer with an unwavering passion for horror. Several of her award-winning feature films have screened worldwide including Obsidian, Mister White, & Loverboy (available on most streaming services.)

Though born and raised in Wyoming, Erica spent most of her life in the swampy American South. She now resides in Connecticut where she works in film and writes and illustrates genre fiction. In her downtime, the bizarre bisexual is typically slathered in garden dirt, kayak fishing, or devouring horror movies with her boyfriend and their Jack Russell *terror*.

Erica also writes spicy romance fiction under the pen name Odessa Alba and cozy mysteries under the pen name Trixie Fairdale.

JOIN THE NEWSLETTER

For news and updates, great discounts, future
bonus material and more, subscribe to the Rusty
Ogre newsletter at:

www.rustyogrepublishing.com

MANTIS

By Erica Summers

An irreverent horror-comedy

Available worldwide in ebook, paperback, jacketed hardcover, and audiobook

Chain-smoking bisexual, Mantis, finds herself amid a demon apocalypse. With the book of Revelations unfurling before her very eyes, she recruits a reformed prostitute, a bubbly stripper, and a hopelessly smitten DJ to try to stop the biblical event in its tracks. Can the uproarious crew of misfit degenerates save the world before it's destroyed?

Locked and loaded with sinister creatures, twisted villains, violent action, and a horny heroine with the charm of a rabid wolverine, Mantis will take you on a hilarious, blood-soaked road trip through the bowels of America's deep south and drop you on the doorstep of the Devil.

From the demented author of Vanity Kills & Bad God's Tower comes a profane, blood-soaked, laugh-out-loud novel full of guts, gore, and good times. A religious, comedic-horror blend of Dogma and From Dusk Til Dawn recommended for fans of Chuck Wendig and Christopher Moore.

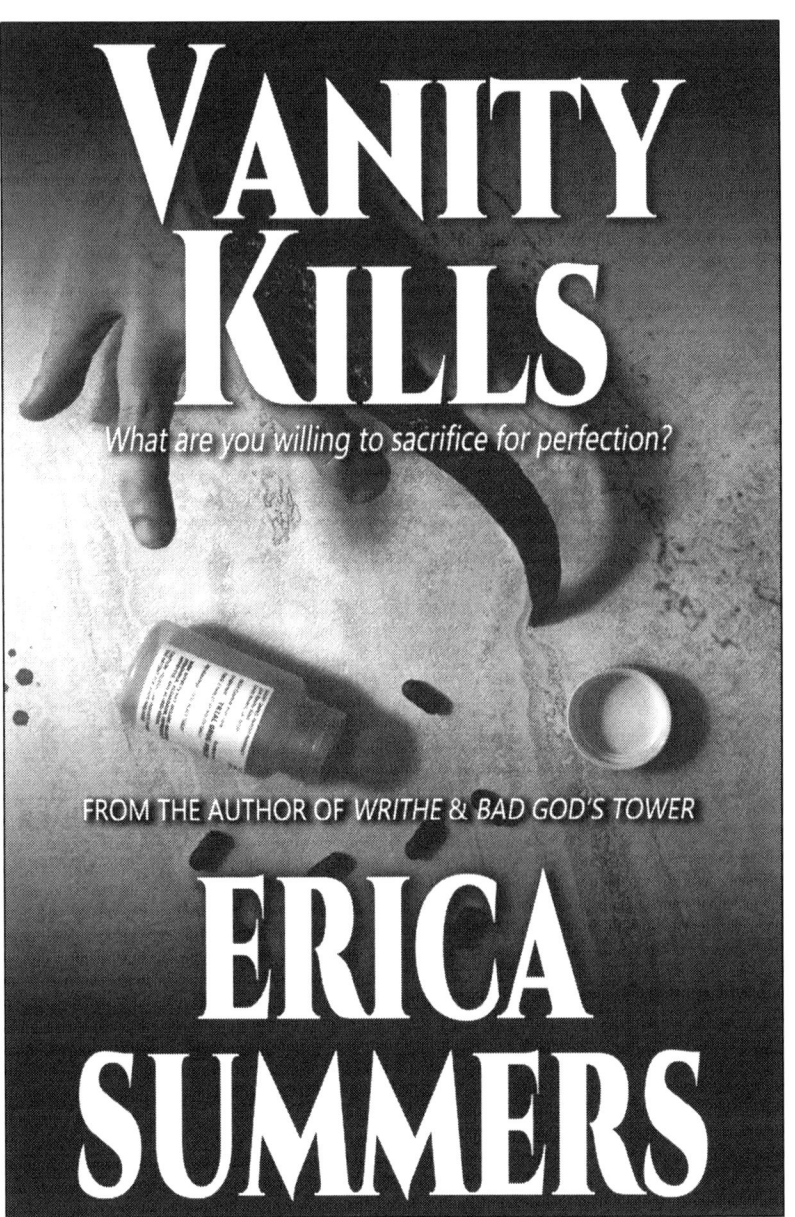

VANITY KILLS

What are you willing to sacrifice for perfection?

FROM THE AUTHOR OF *WRITHE* & *BAD GOD'S TOWER*

ERICA SUMMERS

Vanity Kills
A Medical Thriller/Body-Horror Novel
By Erica Summers

Available worldwide in paperback, ebook, hardcover, and audiobook.

Haunted by his tragic past, Jack LeBlanc, a heavily scarred introvert, finds himself volunteering for the clinical trial of a miraculous new tissue-regeneration drug nicknamed Obsidian. Jack and the other lab rats soon discover that the medication is not what was promised. They're about to find out the hard way that the pills have nightmarish consequences and that Jack's pained conscience isn't the only thing with teeth. With every pill taken, one thing becomes more clear: the path to perfection will be paved with gore.

From the author that brought you Bad God's Tower, DERAILED, and Mantis comes a riveting tale that is part medical thriller, part monstrous body horror that delves into body dysmorphia, narcissism, and conceit as a small ensemble of richly-developed characters embark on a quest for visual perfection that will chill you to the bone. Based loosely on Summers' 2020 feature film, Obsidian, Vanity Kills will have you questioning the side effects of every pill you take.

On a blood-drenched quest for gold,
Eugene and Chester discover a fate far worse than prison

BAD GOD'S TOWER

A WESTERN HORROR NOVELETTE

"...A horror fan's dream.
It's *Funny Games* meets The Descent in the old west."
- Chisto Healy Author of *Two of a Kind* & *The Bucket List*

ERICA SUMMERS

BAD GOD'S TOWER
A Western Horror Novelette
By Erica Summers

Available in paperback, hardcover, e-book, & audiobook

Vicious criminals, Eugene Dempsey and Chester Craven, escape Wyoming Territorial Prison armed with nothing but striped prisoner pajamas and a Lakota's hand-drawn map that, according to legend, will lead them to the unfathomable riches in a secret tunnel burrowed into the base of Devil's Tower. Seeking their golden fortune, the fugitives head north, leaving their dusty trail stained in the blood of innocents.

With two determined buffalo soldiers nipping their heels, the sadistic escapees will soon realize all the gold in the land isn't worth what lies in wait for them in the claustrophobic underground beneath.

LET THE INFESTATION BEGIN.

WRITHE

ERICA SUMMERS
+
H. M. WOHL

A TALE OF HORROR FROM TWO TWISTED SISTERS

WRITHE
An Extreme Horror Novelette
By Erica Summers & H. M. Wohl

Available in paperback, e-book, & audiobook

Garrett was an ordinary New Yorker, appeasing annoying neighbors and paying over-inflated rent for a dumpy apartment in Hell's Kitchen. That is...

Until the larvae hatched.

As the end of the year draws near, Garrett unleashes his violent wrath upon the city of Manhattan. NYPD officers Luca Han and Mel Tredo are on a mission to find the depraved lunatic before he can kill again. Can they capture the homicidal madman in the surging sea of potential victims before the ball drops in Times Square?

Writhe is a hyper-violent, extreme horror novella and is not intended for the faint of heart. This gory splatterpunk tale is brought to you by the twisted real-life sisters behind Vanity Kills, Bad God's Tower, and The Illuminator Saga.

Obsidian (Feature Film)
The award-winning independent feature film version
of *Vanity Kills.*

Streaming on most services.

Only available on DVD & Bluray on the SHOP page of
www.rustyogrepublishing.com

Printed in Great Britain
by Amazon